SHADOW THE CENTAURS

AN ANCIENT GREEK MYSTERY

Look out for the other *Ancient Greek Mysteries* by
Saviour Pirotta, published by Bloomsbury Education.

Mark of the Cyclops
Secret of the Oracle
Pirates of Poseidon

Visit www.bloomsbury.com/education
for more information.

SHADOW OF THE CENTAURS

AN ANCIENT GREEK MYSTERY

SAVIOUR PIROTTA
Illustrated by FREYA HARTAS

BLOOMSBURY EDUCATION

LONDON   OXFORD   NEW YORK   NEW DELHI   SYDNEY

BLOOMSBURY EDUCATION
Bloomsbury Publishing Plc
50 Bedford Square, London, WC1B 3DP, UK

BLOOMSBURY, BLOOMSBURY EDUCATION and the Diana logo are trademarks of
Bloomsbury Publishing Plc

A catalogue record for this book is available from the British Library

ISBN: PB: 978-1-4729-4025-4; ePDF: 978-1-4729-4024-7; ePub: 978-1-4729-4022-3

2 4 6 8 10 9 7 5 3 1

Typeset by Newgen KnowledgeWorks Pvt. Ltd., Chennai, India
Printed and bound by CPI Group (UK) Ltd., Croydon, CR0 4YY

To find out more about our authors and books visit www.bloomsbury.com
and sign up for our newsletters.

For Lauren Paton and Daniel Thomas Paton

CONTENTS

DELPHI

ATHENS

CORINTH

SPARTA

AEGINA

AEGEAN SEA

CRETE

PROLOGUE

Someone at the Gate

Late Winter/Early Spring, 432 BC

It was bitterly cold and the young guard shivered in his flimsy hand-me-down uniform. He was standing at a tower that guarded one of Athens' many city gates. The Acharnian Gate. It looked north over a sprawling suburb crammed with square houses and the rolling countryside of Attica beyond. In the clear moonlight, the young guard could see a road, thin as Ariadne's silken thread, wending its way between orchards and fields. It widened as it approached the city to stop outside the gate.

He stamped his feet on the ground to get some warmth into them. He thought of his younger brother and sister asleep in their straw-lined cots and wished he were at home too, ready to comfort them should they wake up from a distressing nightmare. There'd been a lot of talk in Athens these last few months about a war with Sparta, and his little brother especially had often gone to bed anxious and fearful. Despite his brother's fears, the guard half hoped the rumours were true. Like all men under nineteen, he was not allowed to join in active service. He could only be a guard in Athens, or in one of the many forts guarding the city and the roads leading to it. But if war with Sparta were to be declared, a high-ranking officer somewhere might turn a blind eye to his age and let him join a proper phalanx. All he'd need would be a panoply, the bronze armour that all hoplites wore. If only he could afford one...

'Theodorus!' a gruff voice called from below. 'Would you like some wine to warm your bones?'

'I would, thanks.' The young guard threw one last glance at the empty road and then hurried down a steep flight of stairs. The stairs led to the bottom of the tower, where an older guard sat hunched close to a fire in a brazier. A patched and frequently darned chlamys was pulled tightly around his sagging shoulders. His thick beard was flecked with white, showing he was too old for military duty outside Athens. He nodded at a wine jug on the ground.

'Help yourself.'

'Thank you, Simos. May the gods reward your generosity.' Theodorus picked up the jug and swallowed the wine in large, noisy gulps.

'I'm getting too long in the tooth to be sitting out here in the cold,' grumbled Simos, rubbing his hands together.

'You're retiring soon, aren't you?' said Theodorus.

Simos nodded. 'The wife's family have land close to Mount Parnes. They grow olives and grapes. We'll be joining them in a few months.' He yawned loudly and scratched his armpits.

'You try and get some sleep,' said Theodorus. 'We've been on duty since sunrise. I'll wake you up if we have visitors. Not that it's likely. No one in their right mind will be wandering about in this weather.'

The older man pulled one end of his chlamys over his head and leaned against the brick wall. In no time he was snoring loudly. Theodorus checked that the large wooden beam on the gate was secure. Then he spread his own chlamys close to the fire, placed his spear next to it and removed his helmet. He was tired too…

A loud banging noise made Theodorus wake up with a start.

'Open up, guards!'

'Wait a moment.' Theodorus scrambled to his feet, reaching for his helmet and spear at the same time. He shook Simos awake.

'Are you asleep in there?' demanded the voice outside.

Theodorus ran back up the steps. A large donkey cart had stopped outside the gate. Two figures sat in it, both of them swathed up to the eyes in dark himations. One of them held a bundle on its lap.

'Move away from the gate so I can see you properly,' ordered Theodorus.

The cart trundled back an arm's length.

'State your business,' he said.

'We are delivering cabbages to the priestesses at the temple of Demeter,' replied the cart driver. 'For a dawn sacrifice.'

'No one's allowed into the city at night,' said Theodorus. 'You should know that. You'll have to wait till sunrise.'

'We were held up on the road by a faulty wheel or we would have got here before sunset,' protested the driver.

The other figure held up the bundle, which was now squirming and mewling like a lost kitten. 'For the love of Hera, the mother goddess, our child is sick. We're hoping the priestess will offer a small sacrifice on her behalf when we deliver the cabbages. This cold is doing her no good at all.'

Theodorus turned to Simos, who had come up the steps behind him. 'What are we to do?

On the one hand, we're under orders not to let anyone into the city at night. On the other, there's an ailing child.'

The older guard was about to speak when something came flying over the parapet and landed with a clink at his feet. Theodorus looked down to see a bulging purse on the ground. He picked it up and pulled on the drawstrings. 'There's silver in here, Simos. A bribe. Well, that's made up my mind. Bribes don't work on me.'

'You are not yet a father,' replied Simos. 'Who would blame a man if he is desperate to have his sick child blessed by the goddess?' He chuckled deep in his throat. 'There's enough silver in here for me to buy a few goats and for you to buy a panoply. They'll never make you a fighting hoplite without the proper uniform.'

'Very well,' murmured Theodorus as Simos divided the silver between them. 'But I'm going to check that cart carefully. Just because I've accepted a bribe doesn't mean I'm not going to do my duty.'

He slipped the coins into a pouch tied to his belt, then ran down the steps and removed the wooden beam from the gate. Simos, who had followed him, rushed forward to open it.

The farmer's cart trundled through and the young guard waved it to a halt. The baby whimpered loudly.

'We need to inspect the contents of your cart, sir,' said Theodorus. 'Just a routine check. Nothing to worry about.'

He nodded at Simos, who lit a torch from the brazier and brought it over. The torchlight illuminated four large wicker baskets piled high with cabbages. Theodorus climbed up and rattled them one by one. There seemed nothing suspicious about them. Still, he thought about sticking a spear through one, just to show the farmer who was in charge, but at that moment the sick baby starting wailing and sneezed.

Theodorus jumped back down from the cart. 'Everything's fine, sir,' he called. 'You may be on your way.' The driver flicked the reins and the

cart resumed its journey. It disappeared round the corner.

'I hope we've done the right thing, Simos,' said Theodorus as he helped his friend secure the Acharnian Gate again. 'That man said he was a farmer but he sounded more like a politician at the agora to me. And if he was on his way to the temple of Demeter, he should have turned left at the corner, not right...'

* * *

The farmer's cart trundled up the street till it came to a small shrine dedicated to Hera, where it stopped. The driver climbed down to take a pee behind it. He was a very tall man with weak, narrow shoulders. His belt was tight around an enormous paunch. The other figure on the cart noticed how huge and rough his hands were as he got into the cart and picked up the reins again. They could break your neck in an instant.

'You have done well,' the driver said as the cart started moving again. 'I am most impressed by your skills. My friend was right to recommend you when I said I needed an assistant. You could have fooled me with your act. I'd never have suspected that bundle of rags was not a real baby.'

His companion smiled. 'Thank you, sir. There's nothing to throw a burly guard into a panic like the sound of a sick child. It's called voice-throwing. It's a talent I inherited from my father, who got it from his own father, my late and much-missed grandpa. Everyone in my family is a travelling performer of one kind or another, sir.'

'Do you throw anything else besides your voice?' asked the driver.

'I throw spears, sir, and flaming swords. With deadly accuracy, if I might be permitted to boast a little. Oh, and I throw shadows too.'

'Shadows?' said the driver.

'I make shapes with my hands and I project them on to a wall. It's an art my ancestors learned in India, sir. Believe me, it has saved my life on more than one occasion.'

'I may have use of that particular skill soon,' said the driver.

'Tonight, sir?'

'No, tonight I just needed your help with getting into the city. I will stop the cart on the edge of the Kerameikos, the potter's district. I want you to wait there for me while I retrieve a lost object from a nearby building. But there's another matter.'

The driver's face darkened as he pulled up under an ancient oak tree, and his companion noticed he had only one good eye. The other was made of marble. It glowed in the shadows like a miniature full moon. 'Those guards at the gate certainly fell for your baby trick but I'm not sure I did so well. I let my accent slip for a few moments and I think they suspect I am not the farmer I claim to be. They need to be silenced. Can you help me with that?'

'An arrow through the heart, sir? Perhaps with a fiery head for added effect?'

'Just honest day-to-day kidnap, I think,' laughed the cart driver. 'We don't want to draw attention to our crime. See to it as soon as you can. Those guards will fetch a good price at a slave market in Sparta.'

His companion watched as the driver climbed down from the cart and disappeared into the shadows.

CHAPTER ONE

A Spooky Festival

A few days later

Master Ariston sighed wearily and flopped back on to his couch. 'Those heartless muses refuse to answer my prayers. I can't write any more. Perhaps I should tempt them with an offering of sweet-smelling violets. It is said that the muses can't resist a sacrifice of violets. They love them as much as the people of Athens do. Where in the name of Apollo is Thrax? I need him to fetch me a big bunch of violets right away.'

'You sent him to the market already, sir,' I answered. 'We ran out of dried figs and raisins, remember? You can't write a word without your favourite treats.'

Master Ariston is a travelling poet. He travels all around the Hellenic world performing at weddings, funerals and special parties called symposiums. He is not a very good poet. In fact he's terrible. He only gets hired because his father, Master Lykos, is a retired sea captain with many useful connections in Athenian society.

Thrax is Master Ariston's personal slave. His duties include keeping the master's clothes clean, his footwear polished and his beard trimmed and styled in the latest fashion. He also has to deliver messages, carry Master Ariston's belongings when we are travelling and fetch things from the market. It's lucky that Thrax is very fit or he'd collapse with exhaustion by the end of each day.

I work for Master Ariston too but I am not a slave. I am a free man, a scribe, though if I'm honest, my wages are barely enough to keep me in clean chitons and help out my parents on the island of Kos. My job is to write down all the poems that Master Ariston makes up.

I don't intend to remain a lowly scribe all my life. I have plans to become a famous writer like my hero, Herodotus. He has managed to make dull history read like an adventure story. People will come and listen to me performing my work at grand symposiums. I've written three stories already, based on my adventures with Thrax.

Thrax has his own ambitions, which are bolder and nobler than mine. Like all slaves, he dreams of buying his freedom. Then he'll set off to distant Thrace, where he means to search for his long-lost mother.

Most slaves never get to buy their freedom because it costs more money than they can ever hope to have, but I believe Thrax will soon achieve his ambition. He is my best friend and together we solve mysteries for people who pay us handsomely in return. I always refuse to take my share of the payment, insisting that Thrax needs it more than I do. The stories I get are payment enough for me.

'Nico,' barked Master Ariston, cutting through my thoughts. 'Have you fallen asleep? You haven't written down a word I've said.'

'Sorry, sir,' I said as I picked up my stylus. 'I didn't realise you'd found your inspiration again so suddenly.'

Master Ariston sniffed grandly. 'My dear, if I had to wait for those tight-handed muses to grace me with their presence every time I wanted to write a poem, you'd be out of a job. And I'd be destitute and living on the streets.'

This last claim was a gross lie. Master Ariston doesn't really need to earn money. His family is extremely wealthy. We live with his parents in a beautiful house in Melite, a prosperous deme in the western part of Athens.

I tried not to sigh loudly as we resumed our work.

'Like a rat with a singed tail
The god of war stomps down Mount Olympus
Watch out
His eyes burn like fire.
They will scorch you.'

What utter dross! How I wished Thrax and I had another thrilling mystery to solve. Then I could be figuring out clues and motives in the back of my mind while scratching away on my tablet. It had been just over three months since our return to Athens from the island of Aegina, where we'd had our most exciting and dangerous adventure yet. I'd hoped Athens would soon provide us with another mystery to grapple with. The city was, after all, home to some of the richest and most influential people in the world. And if there's one thing my adventures have taught me it's that wherever there is money and power, there are always criminals plotting some dastardly crime…

'Nico,' chided Master Ariston. 'Your mind is wandering again. Please pay attention.'

I pushed the thought of adventure firmly from my mind. Despite my fervent hopes, it seemed there was not even a sniff of a mystery here, just work. Still, there was *something* to look forward to. It was going to be the Anthesteria in ten days' time.

The Anthesteria is one of four major festivals in Athens. It is so important it has a month named after it, Anthesterion. The festival is dedicated to Dionysus, the god of the grape harvest, wine, theatre and ritual madness. Ritual madness happens when people work themselves up into a frenzy while dancing and feasting at the temple, or during a festival, especially one dedicated to Dionysus. It doesn't last long but people like to boast about how hard the madness gripped them.

I'm not one given to enjoying ritual madness or dancing. Indeed I can barely move without tripping over my own clumsy feet. But I have to admit, I do enjoy a bit of feasting, as can be seen by how tightly my chiton fits around my tummy. I hardly ever drink wine, though, not even at festivals. I prefer to keep my mind clear on grand occasions, so I can observe people whom I might use as characters in my stories.

And there is always a lot to observe during the Anthesteria. For three whole days, the people in Athens celebrate like there's no tomorrow. They hold lavish feasts where the slaves and the domestic staff are invited to sit alongside their masters. The wine from last year's harvest is tasted for the first time and the drinking cups and dishes are bedecked with fresh flowers. There are street parties and competitions that last all night. Relatives visit each other with gifts of food and wine.

But there is a deliciously spooky side to the festival too. It is said that the dead rise from their graves outside the city and float into Athens to celebrate the Anthesteria with their living relatives. People brush tar on their front doors to keep the walking dead out of their houses. They chew on the bitter leaves of the hawthorn so that their foul-smelling breath will stop the ghosts from trying to kiss them and perhaps suck out their souls. The festival ends with a special sacrifice of cooked lentils. It is offered to Hermes, who orders the dead to eat it and then leave the city. No living person touches the cooked lentils, for fear that they will turn into ghosts themselves.

As a budding writer, it was this gruesome side of the Anthesteria that excited me the most. I was looking forward to sharing it with Thrax for the first time. It was the sort of thing he would enjoy.

'Nico,' growled Master Ariston from across the room. 'You are DEFINITELY asleep on the job. Go and splash cold water on your face. I've just had a brilliant idea for a new song and I want you to write it down before I forget it...

'In fair Athens
My fair Athens
There lived a pretty maid
She was tall
And she was fair...'

Master Ariston never finished the song because just then something happened that was to pitch Thrax and me into the most important adventure of our lives, and the most dangerous Anthesteria ever.

There was a soft knock at the door and the front door slave brought in... a skull.

CHAPTER TWO

A Tasteless Invitation

Master Ariston glared at the skull in distaste. 'It's an invitation, master,' said the front door slave. His name was Herakles and his job was to open the front door to visitors and deliver messages around the house. You'd imagine anyone called Herakles would be tall and impressively muscled. Not our Herakles! He was shorter than a ten-year-old child and had the kindest green eyes you could ever imagine. I liked him very much.

'An invitation?' said Master Ariston, sitting up on one elbow. 'The proper way to send an invitation is by word of mouth from a trusted slave. Whoever sent this must be new money. He is ignorant of social etiquette in Athens.'

'Perhaps he is recently arrived from Corinth, sir,' said Herakles. 'I hear they get up to all sort of new-fangled shenanigans there.'

'Who is it from?' said Master Ariston, frowning at the skull as if it were going to leap up and bite him. '*I'm* certainly not going to touch it. Nico, you have a look.'

Herakles brought the skull over to me. It sat on a silver dish and had something poking out of its left eye socket. A rolled-up piece of parchment.

'It's Egyptian papyrus,' I said to Master Ariston as I unrolled it. 'And very expensive too. Whoever sent it definitely has money.'

'And is determined to show it off,' sniffed Master Ariston. 'How hideously common. My father has money but he wouldn't dream of wasting it on skulls and silver dishes.'

I read out the invitation.

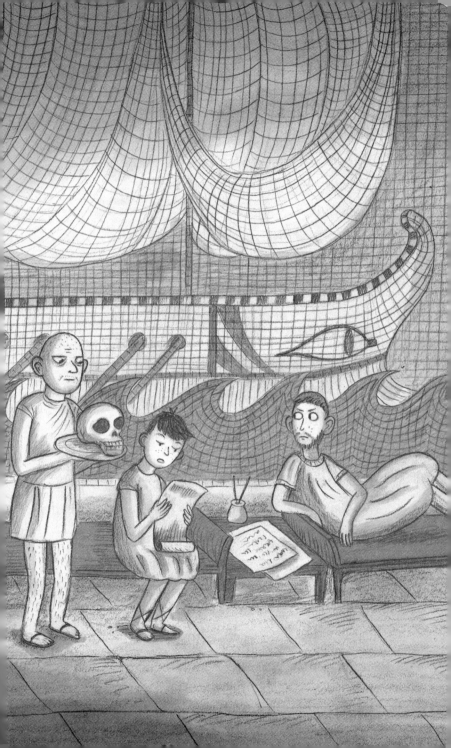

'Menelaus the goat merchant
Requests the pleasure of Master Ariston
  the poet
For a symposium at his house next to the
  shrine of Aphrodite in Kollytos
Tonight after sundown.
There will be a discussion of the underworld
With Socrates the philosopher.
The entertainment will include dancers and
  jugglers in ghostly costumes
Suitable for the approaching festival of the
  Anthesteria.
A carriage will be sent to fetch the master
  and his retinue at sunset.'

Master Ariston looked at me in astonishment. 'Did you say GOAT MERCHANT? Are goat merchants wealthy enough to have symposiums now?'

I rolled up the papyrus. 'Menelaus must be held in great esteem, sir, if the great Socrates himself is going to be there. He is the most highly regarded philosopher in the world. The oracle at Delphi called him "the wisest man alive".'

Master Ariston's lips curled into a contemptuous sneer. 'Socrates is one of those misfits who would attend the opening of a grave if it meant encountering someone to lure into one of his philosophical discussions. I heard he spends hours in the shops around the agora, talking with the young men who are not yet allowed to orate there. He's even interested in slaves' and shopkeepers' views. And his clothes are so stained and bedraggled you'd think he was a penniless farmer. He goes around barefoot, like the lowest of slaves. Can you imagine?' Master Ariston sat back on the couch with a malicious smile on his lips. 'Socrates might be a famous philosopher, my dear, but I hear his wife beats him up almost daily.'

I found this last comment quite shocking. I too had heard rumours that Socrates and his wife often came to blows, but I wouldn't dare make fun of them. In fact I hoped the rumours were just thoughtless gossip. I despise violence of any kind and the sight of someone being beaten leaves me reeling for days. It came to me that perhaps Master Ariston was pointing out

Socrates' difficulties because he was jealous of him. Socrates was famous the world over and I knew that what Master Ariston wanted more than anything else was to be just as honoured and respected.

'Inform the merchant that I'll attend his symposium,' said Master Ariston. 'Perhaps I should meet this man who sells goats for a living but can afford to hold grand symposiums and host the cream of Athens' society. Nico, write a reply on the back of the papyrus. We'll return it in the skull's eye. The right one this time.'

CHAPTER THREE

The Great Socrates

I love Athens. It's the most glorious city in the world. Its temples and public buildings are second to none. It even has a Mint House, where the Athenian coins are struck. I love walking between the columns of the shaded walkways in the agora, the market place, and drinking from its splashing fountains. The walkways are called stoas and provide a cool respite from the hot sun.

But it's not just the magnificent architecture that inspires. The people are pretty special too. If you have any ambition in life, if you want to be an author or an artist, a philosopher or an athlete, this is the place to be. The place to move to. You will always find someone here to help you fulfil your ambition, to make your dream come true.

General Pericles, the first citizen and leader of Athens, is a great admirer of literature and the arts. He rebuilt many of the temples and public buildings that were destroyed during the old wars. When those had been restored, he set about building enough new ones to make Athens the envy of the world. The most awe-inspiring of these stand in an ancient fort on a hilltop inside the city. We call it the Acropolis, and as Master Ariston, Thrax and I rattled past it in Menelaus's carriage that evening we spotted its giant bronze statue of Athena looking out over the city. The setting sun caught the tip of her spear, making it flash like the evening star.

We could see workers and artists crawling all over the roof of a building rising behind the walls of the fort. They were working to finish the decorations of what many thought would be the jewel in the crown of the Acropolis. A temple dedicated to Athena! It was called the Parthenon.

We arrived at Menelaus's house along with many other guests. As is usual with symposiums, only men are invited. They gather in a hall called the andron. Women hold their own gatherings in a part of the house reserved for them, called the gynaikon.

Master Ariston was hoping that the house would be a monument to the bad taste of the newly rich, but the floor of Menelaus's andron was beautifully decorated with a mosaic showing Pan, the protector of shepherds and flocks, in various scenes from myths and legends. Tapestries on the walls depicted him playing hide-and-seek with nymphs.

'I am so glad you could come,' said Menelaus after slaves had washed Master Ariston's feet and he was showing us to a richly decorated couch. 'I hope you will enjoy the evening. Just let me know if something is not to your liking.'

'The man has style, I give him that,' muttered Master Ariston begrudgingly as Menelaus left to greet more guests and a slave brought a three-legged tabled piled high with delicious-smelling food. Thrax and I stared at it hungrily but we knew we would not be offered anything to eat. We were not here as guests but to take care of Master Ariston and make him look important. A second guest soon joined him on the couch.

'Are we to sit together?' he said to Master Ariston. 'I'm sorry I wasn't here to welcome you. I crept out to use the facilities.'

The man was broad-shouldered, with a very thick neck and hairy arms. As he waved at someone crossing the room, I noticed he had callouses on the palms of his hands. He introduced himself as Zeno, the gym master at the agora. 'I am told that Pericles himself might grace us with his presence,' he said. The couch creaked under his weight as he sat down.

'I hear that at every symposium I attend,' sniffed Master Ariston, helping himself to some cubed cheese. 'But he never comes. General Pericles is known to be a very shy man. He prefers to spend his free time studying literature rather than attending symposiums.'

He turned to Thrax and me, standing to attention on his side of the couch. Zeno had not brought any slaves with him. Perhaps he had no need to show off. 'Did you know that Pericles has the biggest forehead in Athens? I've heard he is so embarrassed by it, he always keeps his helmet on. Even in bed!'

Thrax and I threw worried glances at each other. Surely disrespectful talk like this about Athens' first citizen could be considered treacherous?

Zeno coughed loudly to show his own displeasure at the remark. 'I for one think Pericles is the greatest politician in the world. And he doesn't work only on behalf of the nobility and the rich. He looks after the poor too. It's because of him that many hard-working people can rise above their station.'

'Quite,' agreed Master Ariston, completely unaware that his previous comments had caused offence. 'I hear he's letting the masses have free tickets to the theatre. I wonder what the slaves and the goatherds will make of the classics. I shouldn't wonder if they leave them scratching their heads in puzzlement. In my opinion, common people are completely unable to appreciate art.'

I could see Zeno's face turning a bright scarlet at this slight against the poor. He was about to answer Master Ariston when a loud murmur rippled through the andron. The great Socrates had arrived.

'He's actually wearing sandals for once,' gasped Master Ariston, sitting up on the couch and craning his neck to see. 'And he's combed his hair. Wonders will never cease.'

Menelaus himself showed the renowned philosopher to a couch right next to us. I noticed he had a big bruise on the right side of his forehead. My heart sank. Had he been in another fight with his wife? I hoped Master Ariston wouldn't mention it and embarrass us all again. Thankfully, he merely smiled and nodded.

'Good evening,' said Socrates to everyone around him.

'It's a great honour to have you in my house, sir,' said Menelaus, clicking his fingers at a slave who then rushed forward with a basin full of perfumed water to bathe Socrates' feet.

'We usually serve wine after the food but if the great Socrates would like some before, he only has to say.'

'Wine tastes much better when you have to wait for it,' chuckled Socrates. 'I'll nibble on some food like all the other guests for now, thank you.'

Menelaus bowed and left to welcome more guests. Master Ariston nodded at Socrates. 'There are some dried figs on my table, sir. Would you like some? I hear they are your favourite.'

'Thank you,' said Socrates, reaching for the bowl and tucking into a handful of the fruit.

'How is your wife, Xanthippe, sir?' asked Master Ariston.

'Xanthippe is very well, as always,' replied Socrates. 'Although I have to admit that we had another fierce row yesterday and she hurled a vase at my head. She's very good at throwing vases, is my wife.'

'And an accurate shot too, by the looks of it, sir,' said Master Ariston tactlessly.

'And your own lady?' said Socrates. 'Is she a good shot?'

'My name is Ariston, sir,' replied our master. 'I am not yet married.'

'Your father hasn't found you a suitable woman yet, eh?' chuckled Socrates. 'Well, you should marry soon, Ariston. You are not getting any younger. I say every man should marry. A good wife will make him happy. A bad one will make him a philosopher.'

'Do you think women are equal to men, sir?' asked Zeno, leaning forward on the couch.

'Society doesn't treat them as equals,' replied Socrates. 'But if it did, we would soon discover that women are superior to men in most ways.' He turned to Thrax and myself. 'And who, might I ask, are these bright-looking young men?'

'The muscled one is Thrax, my personal slave,' said Master Ariston. 'The chubby one is my scribe. He's called Nico.'

Socrates nodded at Thrax. 'Do you think that women are superior to men, young Thrax?'

'I do indeed, sir,' replied Thrax at once. 'If you compare Hera to Zeus, you'll find that she acts more rationally and kindly than her husband. He's the one who's always getting into trouble and she's the one who always manages to get him out of it.'

'Wise words indeed,' declared Socrates. 'You have a fine slave, Ariston. Treat him well.' He bade Thrax come forward. 'I notice you don't seem to have a fibula, young man. Your chiton is held at the shoulder by a button.' He removed one of many pins on his own rather threadbare clothing. 'Take this as a gift. It will remind you of me when you get into an argument. I have had thousands of arguments in my life and I have never shied away from any of them. That is why I can live with myself.'

'Thank you, sir,' said Thrax, hooking the fibula at his shoulder.

'Thrax is a very intelligent boy,' boasted Master Ariston. 'With the help of Nico, he has solved some fiendish mysteries. He discovered who smashed a precious wedding vase in Corinth and he rescued a girl who'd been kidnapped by dangerous cutthroats in Delphi. He even managed to retrieve a priceless ring stolen by a gang of hoodlums in Aegina.'

'I did hear something about some derring-do in Delphi,' exclaimed Socrates. 'I believe the missing girl is now the pythia at the oracle. So that was you two, was it?' He smiled at Thrax and patted the empty side of the couch. 'Sit here and tell me all about your adventures.'

Master Ariston cleared his throat pompously. 'Sir, if I may remind you, slaves are not permitted to share couches with free men.'

'I don't hold with any of that nonsense,' thundered Socrates. 'Slaves not allowed to sit with free citizens indeed! And the poor boys look hungry to me. Have something to eat, both of you. There's enough here to feed a phalanx. Now, tell me, Thrax, how did you rescue this girl?'

While the slaves kept bringing in more food, Thrax and I took turns in recounting our adventures in Corinth, Delphi and Aegina. There was no time to go into detail but Socrates and Zeno were both clearly impressed.

'You two rival Jason and the Argonauts,' said Zeno.

'Nico has written stories about our adventures,' said Thrax. 'He's a very talented writer.' His praise made me blush but Socrates looked at me again.

'I would like to have a look at your writing. If your master will allow you the time, perhaps you could come to my house and read to me.'

'I can certainly spare him the time,' replied Master Ariston. 'In fact I could bring him to your house myself. I am a writer too, a poet and a singer. I would relish the opportunity to show you some of the poems I am working on.'

'I have great respect for people who can solve mysteries,' said Zeno. 'I am no good at solving anything myself. I've been grappling with a perplexing little mystery of my own these last few days, but I have got nowhere.'

'Oh,' said Socrates, 'what mystery is that?'

'I suspect it is too trivial to interest Thrax and Nico,' replied Zeno. 'It concerns my old slave and my dog.'

'There's no such thing as a trivial mystery, sir,' said Thrax. 'What often appears to be a small matter can often lead to something much bigger – and deadlier.'

'The boy speaks like a true philosopher,' cried Socrates. 'Tell us about your little mystery. We're all ears.'

Zeno was about to speak but just then Menelaus declared the banquet over. Slaves hurried into the andron and cleared away the dirty dishes while others ran in with wine cups of different shapes and sizes. A large vessel called a krater was set in the middle of the room.

'How much wine to water, gentlemen?' called Menelaus. 'Do we want to drink to oblivion or just enough to enjoy the evening's entertainments? We are fast approaching the festival of the Anthesteria and in the spirit of all that is dark and shadowy, we have storytellers to tell us tales of the restless dead, we have dancers who shall dance like shades fleeing from Hades and we have musicians who will play music to make the skin crawl and tantalise the spirit.'

'Three parts water to one of wine,' chorused the guests. 'Let us enjoy the entertainments.'

'Let it be thus,' said Menelaus, as wine and water were poured into the krater. 'And now I invite the great Socrates to take the floor.'

'Come tomorrow to my house,' said Zeno, taking a wine cup. 'I will tell you all about my puzzling dilemma then.'

'I shall come too if I may,' said Socrates as he stood up. 'I am dying to find out if Thrax's words might come true. Will a small mystery lead to a bigger, more dangerous one?'

CHAPTER FOUR

A Very Small Mystery

Zeno's house was right in the middle of a narrow street the locals called the Street of the Four Winds. It ran from one end of the Kerameikos, in the north of Athens, to the other. The house looked small from the outside but once past the altar to Hermes near the front door, Thrax, Master Ariston and I found ourselves in a surprisingly large courtyard with doors all around. Pigeons cooed in a grapevine as we came in. Water gushed in front of an altar dedicated to Ares. Somewhere inside the house a child shrieked and a dog barked happily.

A rather tall slave showed us across the yard into an andron with only two couches. He was an old man, with stooped shoulders and grey bristles sprouting from his ears and nostrils. Socrates had already arrived. We found him sitting on one of the couches, talking excitedly to Zeno and quaffing wine, even at this early hour. A second bruise had joined the first one on his forehead.

'Another flying vase, I'm afraid,' he chuckled sadly as we came in. 'Soon there will be no more pots left in our house and Xanthippe will have nothing to throw when we have a fight.'

'Come in, everyone,' said Zeno. 'Welcome to my andron. Don't stand on ceremony. Take a seat, boys. Hilarion will bring you some snacks and something to drink.

Zeno had obviously just returned home from the gym. He was dressed in the official uniform of the gymnasiarch – a purple cloak and gleaming white boots.

Hilarion took the cloak from him and left to fetch the food and drink. As my eyes adjusted to the gloom, I could see a rather gruesome mosaic on the floor. It showed a battle between centaurs and soldiers. The hulking centaurs wielded enormous clubs with sharp spikes and tree branches. The men looked just as deadly, the tips of their spears tearing into centaur flesh. There seemed to be blood everywhere, worked out in polished crimson tesserae. In the background, women and children dressed for a grand occasion were screaming.

'It shows the famous battle between the Lapith people and the centaurs,' said Socrates. 'It took place at the wedding of the Lapith king, Pirithous, and his bride, Hippodamia. She was a famous horse-trainer who could put any horse under her spell.'

'I know the legend well,' said Master Ariston. 'The Lapiths were a brave people who lived in the region of Thessaly. They managed to drive the centaurs away and the creatures were banned from ever setting foot in their country.'

'It is a hideous work of art,' admitted Zeno, noticing the horrified look in my eyes. 'I don't know what makes people commission such frightful mosaics. My wife Penelope won't let my son in here until I have it replaced with something more gentle and wholesome. She says it will give him nightmares.'

'I would have had it removed a long time ago,' said Master Ariston with a shudder. 'I agree with your wife, sir. It can't be good for a child to look at this kind of thing.'

'Zeno and his family have only lived in this house a short time, master,' Thrax explained. 'They haven't yet had time to tear up the mosaic.'

Zeno's head swivelled round on his thick neck. 'By the sacred cloak of Herakles, you are right, my boy. How did you guess we've only just come to live here?'

'The boy doesn't guess, my dear,' chuckled Socrates. 'He deduces.'

'Deduces?'

'Yes, deduces,' laughed Socrates. 'It means drawing conclusions from the evidence around you.'

'Well, how did you deduce it then?' Zeno asked Thrax.

Thrax looked around him. 'There are clues everywhere you look, sir. The shrine in the courtyard, for example. It's dedicated to Ares, the god of war. The man who lived here before you was a soldier. You are a gym master. I expect one day you will remove Ares and replace him with Herakles, the god of sports and protector of athletes.'

Zeno's mouth opened and shut like a fish's. 'The boy's right,' he mumbled. 'I have already commissioned a sculptor to make me a statue of Herakles.'

'And then I noticed there are no curtains in the doorways,' continued Thrax. 'You moved here from a smaller house with lower doorways. The curtains need altering.'

'By the golden bolts of Zeus,' exclaimed Zeno. 'The boy is right again.'

Hilarion shuffled in with cups and pitchers. He set them down stiffly, without a word, and left the andron again. Zeno poured wine for the adults and water for Thrax and myself.

'So this is the mystery I have for you,' he said, when he had our full attention. 'It's only a little one, as I warned yesterday, but I've been puzzling it over ever since it happened. If you boys can solve it, there'll be a handsome reward for you both.'

He sipped noisily from his wine cup and began.

'My wife has a dog, a Melitan called Argos after Odysseus's beloved pet.'

'An ironic choice of name for a small lapdog like a Melitan,' chuckled Socrates. 'Your Penelope has a sense of humour, sir.'

'I adore Melitans,' interrupted Master Ariston. 'They're so soft and fluffy you just want to give them a cuddle. I longed to have one when I was a child but my father would not hear of it. He thinks dogs are only for guarding houses against intruders and Melitans are too small to guard anything.'

'Penelope is devoted to hers,' continued Zeno. 'She offers sacrifice on its behalf at the household altar, and she lets the wretched thing lick her dish clean after she's finished eating. My son is equally smitten. He won't go to sleep at night unless Argos curls up next to him in his cot. I'm not so fond of the thing myself. It yaps incessantly at everything that moves and I spend a small fortune on titbits for it. Fresh meat and fish. It won't eat anything else. And it was getting fat. Recently a friend of my wife's told her that dogs benefit from exercise just as much as we humans do. So now Hilarion walks the dog every time he goes to the market. We even bought the thing a collar and lead so it would not stray and get lost.

'The other night Hilarion was on his way home with Argos when someone leaped on him from a shadowy doorway and thumped him on the back. Poor Hilarion had change in his mouth and nearly choked on the coins. He was bent double, trying to cough up the money, when the assailant grabbed Argos's lead and ran off with the dog. Hilarion stumbled to his knees and I'm sure he would have choked to death right there on the street had not a kind passer-by come to his rescue and given him a second thump that actually made him swallow the coins.'

'Goodness,' interrupted Master Ariston. 'I shall never carry money in my mouth again. I'll insist Thrax or Nico do it for me.'

'The kind passer-by helped Hilarion home, where the slave managed to bang on the front door before passing out from shock,' continued Zeno. Penelope was inconsolable when she realised Argos had been kidnapped. She sent me and Olympos, one of our other slaves, to look for it. Alas, we could not find the dog anywhere. I determined to go to the police in the morning – but here's the thing. When Hilarion opened the front door at dawn, he found Argos sitting patiently on the doorstep.'

'The brave fellow managed to escape from his heartless kidnappers,' cheered Master Ariston. 'He really does deserves his heroic name. Long live Argos!'

'Oh no,' said Zeno. 'Argos didn't escape. Someone had brought him back. His lead was tied securely to the door handle. That's the conundrum that's been keeping me awake. What would make a thief steal a dog only to return it? It just doesn't make sense. If for some reason the thief changed his mind, why risk bringing Argos back? Why not let the dog loose to find his own way home? Or sell him and make some money? I hear there is a buoyant trade in stolen pets, especially pure breeds like Argos.'

'Perhaps a kind neighbour found him and brought him back,' suggested Master Ariston.

'I've asked the neighbours,' replied Zeno. 'It wasn't any of them. And if a stranger somehow knew where Argos lived, they wouldn't have left him tied to the door where he could have been stolen again. They would have knocked on the door to let us know he'd been found. No, it *had* to be the thief who brought him back.'

Socrates turned to Thrax. 'What do you make of it, young man?'

Thrax replied without hesitation. 'I can see right away why the dog was stolen, sir. But I don't think that was the only crime committed against Zeno and his family that night. I believe a second one occurred, right here, in this house.'

CHAPTER FIVE

Argos

'A second crime.' Zeno sounded impressed. 'Why do you say that? There are no clues as far as I can see.' He paused for a moment. 'Your master is right, you are exceedingly clever.'

'We underestimate the young,' chimed in Socrates, raising his wine cup at Thrax and myself. 'As we underestimate the poor and indeed the honest craftsman. These people have a lot to teach the rich and the privileged if only they would listen.'

'I would love to investigate some more, sir,' said Thrax.

'By all means, young man,' said Zeno. 'Please find out what you can. Without neglecting your duties to Master Ariston, of course. I will pay you triple what I intended if there really was a second crime.'

'I do not work alone, sir,' said Thrax. 'Nico assists with my investigations, and his help is invaluable.'

'Not that I am looking for money,' I said hurriedly. 'I enjoy helping Thrax, and writing about our adventures is payment enough for me.'

'When will you have some answers?' asked Zeno.

'I do not know yet, sir,' replied Thrax, 'but, with Master Ariston's permission, Nico and I will start our investigations right away. I take it you have not noticed anything out of the ordinary recently?'

Zeno shook his head. 'Like what?'

'Strangers lurking on your street,' said Thrax. 'Anything in the house gone missing.'

'Hilarion might be a doddery old man,' sniffed Zeno, 'but he has eyes like a hawk. He'd have spotted anyone dawdling outside the door, and would have informed me at once. And nothing's gone missing from the house. We don't have much to steal anyway. I am comfortably off but I do not spend much on myself. I prefer to help pay for public festivals and rituals at the temple,'

'Spoken like a true Athenian,' murmured Master Ariston, who much preferred hoarding his own money to giving it away to the public coffers.

'How many of you live here?' asked Thrax.

'There's me, my wife and my son,' replied Zeno. 'My wife has her own personal slave, a Jewish girl called Deborah. She's away at the moment, visiting relatives. Hilarion looks after the house even though he's getting on in years. There's a third slave I've already mentioned, Olympos. He helps Hilarion with the heavy cleaning and the carrying, and he acts as my personal slave when I need to appear at official functions with one. My wife has sent him fishing today, so he's not here. And there's Eirene the cook. She rarely comes out of the kitchen, poor thing. Won't say boo to a goose. A very timid woman though an excellent cook.'

'Can we meet Argos, sir?' said Thrax.

'Certainly.' Zeno called for Hilarion and the slave fetched the dog. It was a gorgeous little creature, its muzzle and pointy ears very much like a small wolf's. Its fluffy coat was white as Delphian snow. Master Ariston started cooing the moment he saw it.

'Oh, but he's adorable,' he said, sitting forward on his couch and holding out his hand for the dog to lick.

Argos barked ferociously and snapped at Master Ariston's fingers. Master jumped back, pretending not to mind. The dog eyed a dish of nuts on a three-legged table. He whimpered hungrily.

'You can see why Hilarion has to walk him every day,' chuckled Zeno. He threw some nuts across the andron for the dog to catch. 'Get 'em, boy. Get 'em.'

The dog caught the nuts, then trotted over to Zeno and gave his knee a big, friendly lick as if to say thank you. He licked Thrax's knee too, wagging his furry tail enthusiastically.

'He seems to like *you*,' grunted Master Ariston with a hint of childish envy in his voice.

Thrax gathered Argos gently in his arms and let the dog lick his face. He inspected the collar. 'I take it this is the same collar Argos was wearing when he was kidnapped, sir.'

'It is indeed,' said Zeno. 'It's quite an expensive one apparently. A friend of my wife's bought it on a visit to Egypt.'

'Do I have permission to search your house if and when I need to, sir?' asked Thrax.

The gym master nodded. 'Of course. I know an honest boy when I see one. I trust you and your friend implicitly.'

'Thank you,' Thrax replied politely. 'I understand you are attending a performance at the agora tonight, sir?'

'I am indeed,' gasped Zeno while Hilarion led Argos out of the andron. 'Though I haven't said as

much while you were here. How did you guess…
I mean how did you *deduce* that was the case?'

Socrates chuckled. 'Even I could work that one out, Zeno. There's a delicious aroma wafting through the house. Your cook is making honey cakes, the perfect food to give to your friends at a festival. I take it you are going to watch the acrobats from Sparta. Everyone in Athens knows they are performing in the agora tonight. It's one of the spectacles commissioned by Pericles in honour of the Anthesteria.'

'There's going to be more than acrobats,' said Master Ariston. 'I heard there will be tightrope walkers who perform right above the audience. There's even a magician who projects hand-shadows on a wall. He's pretty impressive from what I've been told, although some purists find his art a bit too foreign for their tastes. Apparently he can create all sorts of mythical creatures just by wiggling his hands in front of a flaming torch. Dancing nymphs and all that. No one knows how he does it. He hides behind a curtain with his assistant and the audience can only see the moving shadows on the wall, large as titans. I'd love to go and watch but my father insists I stay at home tonight. We have friends coming round for dinner and he wants me to entertain them.'

'I assume you will take Hilarion with you, sir,' said Thrax to Master Zeno.

The gym master nodded. 'Of course. Olympos won't be home in time. Besides, it will do Hilarion good to go out at night again. He's been very skittish since the assault and he needs to regain his confidence.'

'May I ask that you take Argos with you too, sir?' said Thrax.

Zeno raised a quizzical eyebrow but nodded. 'I shall have to ask my wife to make sure the door to the gynaikon is securely locked, then. Argos might be small but Ariston's father is wrong about Melitans. They make fierce guard dogs. Penelope feels safer with him around when I'm not in.'

'Thank you, sir.'

Zeno rose from the couch, indicating that our meeting was over. Hilarion shuffled back into the andron to clear away the cups and bowls.

Zeno laid a hand on Thrax's shoulder. I suspect he wanted to shake his hand but he couldn't because Thrax was a slave. 'I'm really looking forward to finding out how you and your friend solve this case, young man. May Athena, the goddess of wisdom, assist you. And Hilarion here will ask Cook to give you some of her honey cakes before you leave. They are truly delicious.'

CHAPTER SIX

A Meeting

As soon as we left Zeno's house, Thrax and I made straight for our private meeting place.

In every adventure we've had, Thrax has always insisted we have secret meetings where we can discuss the mystery in hand, take notes and plan our next move. In Corinth, we met in a small courtyard overgrown with vines. In the sacred city of Delphi, Thrax built a tree house in the branches of an ancient olive tree. On the island of Aegina, we held meetings in a forgotten hut at the back of a ruined house. For this mystery, we didn't have to look for a new meeting place. We already had one.

A year before Thrax came to live with us, I had discovered an ancient tree in a lane behind our house. It was gnarled and twisted, a mighty oak, sacred to both Zeus and Pan. They say the rustling of its leaves is really the voice of Zeus, whispering in a mysterious language. I climbed into the branches to hear the god better and discovered the tree was hollow. It didn't take me long to turn it into my own secret hideaway.

In its damp-smelling darkness I kept my few secret and precious belongings. An old stylus my mother had given me, a toy wooden horse my father carved for me when I was still a toddler, a few good-luck pebbles I had found on a beach. And, of course, a small supply of dried fruit and nuts.

I can't write or even concentrate if my tummy is rumbling with hunger. My little store, which I keep in a pottery jar with a tight-fitting lid, has often kept me going in lean, unhappy times.

When Thrax came to live with us, we transformed the hideaway into a proper secret meeting place. We mended two broken stools we found on a scrapheap. I dug up two old himations to drape over our legs when it got cold and Thrax supplied an old goatskin that we filled with water to drink along with the nuts and dried fruit.

I checked to make sure no one could see us, before I followed Thrax into the branches of the tree and dropped feet-first into our meeting place.

We'd only just eaten the delicious honey cakes but I was ready for some nuts and dried figs. I opened the jar. Thrax took the stool opposite me.

'I declare this meeting open,' he said, reaching inside his chiton and taking out a medallion showing the face of the Medusa. 'Long live the Medusa League.'

I had a similar medallion hanging on a leather thong around my neck. 'Long live the Medusa League,' I repeated, holding it up.

The Medusa League is a secret society that Thrax and I started after we solved our first mystery. Its members are people we have met on our adventures. First to join us were Fotini and her slave girl Gaia. They live in the city of Corinth. Selene, who became the pythia at the oracle in Delphi, is also a member, as are Alexa and Smilis, two children we rescued from pirates near the island of Aegina. They are all brave heroes without whom we would never have survived our adventures. Like us, they each wear the medallion of the Medusa around their neck and Thrax and I know we can rely on their help should we ever need it again.

I opened my tablet and spat on the point of my stylus to clean it, ready to take notes. Thrax reached in the jar for a few raisins and chewed on them thoughtfully.

I did the same. 'I've been racking my brains all the way here but I can't for the life of me think why the dog was stolen,' I said through a big mouthful or raisins. 'Or why it was returned.'

Thrax smiled. 'Zeno himself gave us the clue.'

'Did he?'

'Remember what he said about Argos?'

'He said he yaps too much. He doesn't sound very fond of him.

'Which isn't true at all,' chuckled Thrax. 'Dog and master have an excellent relationship. You can tell by how affectionately Zeno talked to Argos when he threw him the nuts, and the way Argos licked Zeno's knee. Only a dog who loves and trusts his master does that.'

'But why hide his affection for the dog?' I wondered.

'Big men like Zeno are not supposed to like small fluffy creatures like Melitans. They consider them a woman's pet,' replied Thrax. 'Real men prefer big hulking dogs like Molossians. But what else did he say about Argos, when I suggested he take him to the agora tonight?'

'He said that he'd have to get his wife's permission…'

'Because?'

I ate a dried fig to help me remember. 'Because Penelope feels safer having the dog at home when her husband is out.'

'Exactly,' said Thrax. 'He said Argos is a first-rate guard dog. I agree with him. We had a Melitan on the farm outside Thebes and it barked the place down if someone dared as much as come up the meadow to the front door. Melitans are descended from wolves and they have their alertness and confidence. So what do you conclude from Zeno's comment?'

I chewed on two more figs and thought very hard. 'Someone… wanted the dog out of the way?'

'Good thinking. Someone wanted Argos out of the way for the night, so they could break in without alerting Zeno and his family. They returned him in the morning after the crime had been successfully carried out.'

'But Zeno insists nothing in the house has gone missing.'

'Nothing that he's noticed,' said Thrax.

'Are you saying a thief broke into the house and stole something that Zeno didn't know was there?'

'That's my theory at the moment,' said Thrax. 'I guess there's only one way to find out.' He placed the lid on the fruit jar to stop me from eating any more. 'Let's sneak out later. In the first hour of the night. We're going on a very special mission, Nico. Bring a lamp and make sure you wear your darkest himation.'

CHAPTER SEVEN

The Golden Helmet

It was quite dark when Thrax and I slipped out of Master Lykos's house. It had been a busy evening for both of us. Master Ariston had ordered me to copy four especially long poems on to papyrus, which he wanted to gift to his father's guests at the symposium.

After that, both Thrax and I were required to attend to Master Ariston while he entertained with his songs and also joined in the merry-making. Sometimes Master Lykos's symposiums can be tedious affairs, with rich merchants sitting around drinking and discussing business. The wine is heavily mixed with water so that no one gets drunk. Not so tonight. With the Anthesteria just over a week away, Master Lykos had banned any mention of work.

Strictly speaking my job is to write down any poems or songs Master Ariston makes up during a performance. But tonight, he twice ran out of fried eel and sent me to fetch more from the kitchen. Master Ariston often forgets that I am a free man, a trained scribe, and that it's not my duty to run errands.

For a while it seemed like we would never be able to start our investigations, but then some athletes arrived late. They had already been to another gathering and were red in the face as they tumbled into the andron. They suggested a game of kottabos, which is particularly popular with the rich and famous in Athens. But it's a sport I truly dislike. The players fling the dregs from their wine cups at a statue on a pole, trying to knock a discus out of its hand.

Master Ariston flapped his hands at Thrax and me. 'Take the rest of the night off, boys. I have a feeling it's going to get very messy in here with all this wine flying around. I would leave too, but my father insists on me staying till the bitter end. It'll be dawn by the time I get to bed.'

'Where are we going, Thrax?' I asked, as we changed out of our party chitons and put on our himations.

Thrax wasn't very forthcoming. 'You'll see.'

We heard loud cheering as we passed through the agora, and saw lights dancing on the columns of the southern stoa, which also served as a market place. I would have liked to stay and watch some of the entertainment but Thrax urged me on. He waved to a short boy who was sitting near a fountain, tucking into an enormous loaf of bread.

'Hello, Akademus! That bread any good?'

'Hard as an altar stone,' replied Akademus, standing up and falling in step beside us. 'Still it's free, I suppose. The bread seller is dead on his feet. I could have carried away his entire stall and he wouldn't have noticed. Long live the Anthesteria.'

'Well, you take care,' warned Thrax. 'There are lots of policemen about.'

Akademus treated us to a toothless grin. 'They're too slow to catch me.' And a moment later he had melted into the crowd.

'I suppose that's one of your new friends,' I said to Thrax as we approached the potters' district. Thrax had been making friends with a lot of street urchins since we had got back to Athens. They weren't the kind of boys I would have chosen to be friends with. Indeed, I kept well away from them whenever I came across them, assuming they would taunt me or bully me right there in the street. Thrax insisted he was just keeping an eye on them. No one in the city seemed interested in their welfare. And their friendship might come in useful one day, he pointed out. They knew every hidden corner of Athens and they were teaching Thrax a lot of new skills.

'What kind of skills?' I asked.

'Not the kind you'd learn from a well-paid tutor.' He laughed. 'Learning how to spot a cheat at games. Sending secret messages by imitating the call of birds. That sort of thing.'

The Kerameikos was completely deserted. Everyone seemed to be down at the agora, enjoying the performance. The Anthesteria is especially popular with the working people of Athens and they jump at the chance to extend the celebrations beyond its three days.

Thrax stopped outside Zeno's house.

'We're going inside here?' I asked.

'Yes, we're going to search Zeno's andron for clues.'

'But why do we have to come secretly at night? Zeno gave us permission to search the house whenever we want.'

'We don't want to alert anyone who might tamper with the evidence.'

I had no idea who that 'anyone' might be and I knew that this was not the time to ask Thrax. We huddled behind an altar to Zeus across the street and examined Zeno's house, looking for a way in.

Despite its fame and importance, Athens is not a large city. There is not much space for private orchards and gardens. Most houses, even those of the rich and powerful, tend to be squashed together in long rows. They are plain on the outside, possibly with an altar dedicated to Hermes outside the front door. Zeno's was no different. It had two tiny windows above the front door (some houses have none), which was daubed with a huge patch of tar to scare away the ghosts of the Anthesteria.

'Those windows are too high to reach even if we could clamber up the wall,' I said.

A rosy light shone through the slats on the wooden shutters, warning us that the rooms were occupied.

'That must be the women's quarters,' said Thrax. 'Anyone going up there would have to get past Penelope or her slave Deborah, if she's back.'

'Perhaps the thief got in through the smoke-hole in the kitchen roof,' I suggested.

Nico shook his head. 'There's no smoke, look. Zeno must have an old-fashioned kitchen with a window to let the cooking smoke out into the yard.'

'Maybe the intruders climbed up the walls and jumped down into the yard, then.'

'The walls are too high for that,' said Thrax. 'And too smooth to scale.'

'Perhaps they managed to open the front door.'

'It's locked as securely as a city gate at night. The slaves put a wooden beam across it. I checked this morning. Let's try the back.'

We walked to the end of the street and turned into a narrow lane. To our right the walls of the city rose high and mighty, casting a shadow on the houses. To our left, chicken coops and rabbit hutches stood outside the back doors. It was eerily silent.

'This reminds me of my parents' back yard,' I said. 'They share it with their neighbours and I used to spend a lot of time there playing with my friends. Pity this lane hasn't got the same happy feeling. Perhaps it's because I know there's a vast graveyard on the other side of the wall. It makes the place feel, well, a bit haunted and spooky, especially now that the Anthesteria is so near. I can just imagine ghosts floating through the walls in search of their relatives in Athens.'

At first glance, Zeno's house seemed just as impenetrable at the back as at the front. There was a narrow door, also daubed with tar. Zeno and his wife were taking no chances with the ghosts of the Anthesteria. A round mosaic of a snake-haired Medusa grinned down at us from above the lintel. A tiny bird slept in a reed cage hung next to it. Thrax looked for a door handle but there was none. There was not even a lock with a keyhole. The door could only be opened from inside.

'I'm flummoxed,' I whispered. 'How *did* the intruder get in?'

Thrax stepped back from the door and looked around. Even in the shadows, I could see his eyes were narrowed. He was concentrating.

'Of course,' he said after a while. 'The way in is staring us straight in the face. Look around you again, Nico. What do you see?'

'A door with no handle,' I whispered back. 'And a cage with a sleeping bird in it. It might be a tame swallow.'

'And what else?'

'A chicken coop by the back door,' I said. 'It's made of wood and reeds. The chickens in it are fast asleep. They're a bit on the small side.'

'That's because they're not chickens,' Thrax corrected me. 'They're quails. Men like Zeno eat a lot of quails' eggs to make their muscles bigger. Look at the coop again. Now what do you see?'

I peered closely. 'There are six quails in all, huddled together for warmth.'

'Look *past* the birds, Nico.'

'There's a square hole in the wall,' I said.

'It lets the birds go indoors when it's raining,' said Thrax. 'I bet you that's how the intruder got in. Shall we see if I'm right?'

'I don't think I could fit through that hole,' I said uneasily.

'You don't have to. I'll go. You just wait here for me.'

Thrax opened the door to the coop without making a sound and crept in on all fours. The quails clucked softly in their sleep as he wormed his way through the straw and the square hole. But none of them so much as stirred. I had to give it to

Thrax, he was more slippery than a snake in the grass. I waited in the shadows for what seemed like a year, praying to the gods that no one would come out of a nearby house and see me. Then I heard a creak and the back door opened.

'Come on in, Nico.'

I followed Thrax inside and he closed the door gently behind us. I felt straw under my feet and smelled the rank stench of bird droppings. As my eyes got used to the dark, I could see amphorae stacked against one wall. Dried sausages and bunches of onions hung from hooks in the ceiling. A few hens sat asleep on the amphorae. This was a storeroom.

Thrax opened a second door in the far wall and I slipped behind him into a kitchen. A round figure – Eirene, I guessed – lay under a himation close to a smouldering bread oven. Her snoring shook the room and her enormous bosom rose and fell to the rhythm of it.

I tiptoed after Thrax through yet another door, my heart beating embarrassingly loudly in my chest. This one led out into the yard.

'Light your lamp at the altar, Nico,' said Thrax.

I did as he asked and hurried after him into the andron. In the faint light of my little lamp, the mosaic on the floor looked even more gruesome. The red tesserae glowed like freshly spilled blood. The centaurs grinned with lethal, pointed teeth.

Thrax closed the door behind us. 'I reckon we have almost an hour before the performance at the agora ends and Zeno brings Argos back home.'

'What kind of clue are we looking for?' I whispered.

Thrax stood by the closed door and surveyed the room. 'I don't know, but I have a feeling this awful mosaic holds the key to the mystery. Help me move the couches.'

We moved the couch closest to the door and I winced as its legs scraped loudly against the mosaic. Thrax went down on his knees to examine the floor. There wasn't much to see, just the bottom part of the mosaic, a swirl of dark rocks and moss picked out in muddy green. We dragged the couch back into place.

Above us, we heard footsteps thumping across the floor, followed by a crash and the sound of a child howling. I imagined Zeno's son must have blundered into a piece of furniture, or tripped over his amis, his chamber pot. The soothing voice of an adult woman calmed him down.

'We're right under the gynaikon,' muttered Thrax. 'We need to be really quiet. Come on, Nico, help me shift the other couch.'

We pushed the second couch aside, this time to reveal the top end of the mosaic. I brought the lamp closer and we both saw the head of a furious-looking centaur. He had bright yellow eyes with narrowed pupils. His shiny hair was swept back from his wide forehead in a swirl of dark tesserae. His beard was long and curled. In his hands a lethal-looking club – the centaurs' weapon of choice – bristled all over with glistening spikes. It made my skin crawl just looking at him.

Unlike the other four-legged beasts in the mosaic, who were bare-chested, this centaur had a wine-coloured chlamys swirling around his shoulders. Perhaps he was a leader of some kind, or even a king. I thought of the ancient legend.

'Nico!' Thrax interrupted my thoughts. 'Look at the centaur's fibula.'

I hovered my lamp over the beast's chlamys. The pin holding it to his hairy shoulder was shaped like a lambda, the eleventh letter of our alphabet. It was formed out of golden tesserae.

'It sort of looks like a helmet, with a pointy top,' I said.

'It does,' agreed Thrax. The golden fibula flashed in the lamplight and I stared at it mesmerised as Thrax ran his fingers over it.

'The golden tesserae are slightly raised,' he said, pressing on them. He spread his fingertips, like a shepherd putting his fingers on the holes of a reed pipe, and pressed harder. There was a grating sound and a square section of the mosaic moved sideways, revealing a dark hole.

'Eureka!' Thrax took the lamp from me and held it down into the hole. We made out a flight of steps, leading down into the darkness. 'Follow me, Nico,' he whispered.

CHAPTER EIGHT

A Marble Sarcophagus

We picked our way down the steps, which were slippery with mould. They led to a vault no bigger than a child's bedroom. Our heads almost scraped against the low ceiling as we stood looking around. There was an overpowering smell of rot and I could see the walls were glistening with condensation. They were hewn out of solid rock, the marks of the mason's pickaxe still visible through the stained, peeling whitewash.

'This was probably a shelter from pirates and marauders,' I said. 'It would have been used hundreds of years ago when Athens was still vulnerable to pirate attacks. Whole families would have hidden in here to evade being kidnapped. Look!'

I held up my lamp to illuminate graffiti scratched on the wall. They showed a pirate ship approaching a harbour. On the shore was a house with stick figures of people inside it. Their hands were held together in prayer to Hera, the mother goddess, who hovered protectively on a cloud above the house.

'People must have carved these as a form of sacrifice while they were locked up in here,' I said to Thrax.

'This place might have started out as a shelter,' said Thrax. 'But someone more recently used it as a treasure vault.'

I lowered the lamp and we spotted a row of three wooden chests. Their planks were rotten, the lids crawling with slugs.

'Do you think the intruder broke into Zeno's house to come down here, looking for treasure?' I asked.

'I'm pretty sure there's none here now, but we'll soon find out.' Thrax tried lifting one of the broken lids but it fell to bits in his hands. The chests were empty.

I turned to examine the rest of the vault but there was nothing that gave me a clue as to what the intruder could have taken.

'Hey, Nico, look at this.' Thrax had picked his way across the slimy floor to where a small shrine was carved into the wall. There had been the statue of a god in it once but someone had smashed it, leaving just a pair of marble feet on the base. In front of the broken statue lay a miniature sarcophagus, shaped like a tortoise with its head inside its shell. The body of it was made of marble but the lid was a real tortoise shell, no bigger than my hand. Thrax tried to pick it up but the feet were glued firmly to the stone.

'I've seen sarcophagi like these for sale at the agora,' I said, 'though none of them were as fine as this one. I believe they are imported from Egypt, where rich people are buried with their

mummified pets. It must have cost a lot of money. Do you think there are the remains of a tortoise still inside it?'

Thrax discovered the shell opened like the lid on a perfume pot. The sarcophagus was empty.

'Whatever the intruder took from the vault, I think it must have been in here,' he said. 'Nico, bring the lamp closer.'

He bent his head over the sarcophagus as I held the lamp over it.

'There, look.' I peered at the marble. In the lamplight, I could make out a faint handprint.

'You're right,' I said.

'The thief must have looked in the chests before opening this. He transferred mould from them to the tortoise. Very clumsy of him and very lucky for us. Not that he expected anyone to find their way down here, let alone examine this creepy shrine.'

Just then the lamp guttered, throwing wild shadows across the shrine. The oil was running out.

'Zeno and Hilarion are going to be back at any moment,' said Thrax. 'Let's get out of here while we still have some light.'

The lamp decided to go out just as the secret panel slid shut, hiding the entrance to the vault. We replaced the couch back against the wall and were stealing across the yard when a dog started barking ferociously outside the front door. It was Argos. Master Zeno and Hilarion were home.

'Run for it, Nico,' hissed Thrax, pulling his himation over his head. 'We may still be able to get out unnoticed.' I charged after him into the kitchen where a confused-looking Eirene was hastily rubbing the sleep out of her eyes. She let out a blood-curdling scream when she spotted us.

'Ghosts! Help! Ghosts!'

We made a dash for the back door, waking up the roosting hens, which squawked in alarm. We stumbled out into the lane just as Argos burst into the storeroom, barking loud enough to wake the dead on the other side of the city wall. How such a small animal can make such a loud noise, I'll never know.

Thrax slammed the door shut and neither of us stopped running until we reached the safety of the agora. It was still full of people, talking excitedly about the magician's hand-shadow performance.

'Do you think Eirene would recognise us if she saw us again?' I asked Thrax, leaning against a column to catch my breath. I am not used to running and I had a terrible stitch in my side. My ankles were on fire.

'Didn't you hear the woman?' giggled Thrax. 'She thought we were ghosts invading the house for the Anthesteria. The others will convince her she was just having a nightmare.'

The food stalls in the agora were doing a brisk late-night trade. I dug into my purse for loose change and treated us to a hot sausage each. 'It's a pity we didn't have time to explore the secret vault a bit more,' I said as we sat in a stoa to eat.

'I think we did extremely well,' said Thrax. 'I know *exactly* what the intruder took from the sarcophagus.'

'Is that the end of the case, then?' I said. 'Do we just tell Zeno what was taken and ask for payment?'

'We can hardly expect the man to take us for our word,' Thrax replied. 'We have to retrieve the stolen object as irrevocable proof. Which is not going to be easy. I don't think this is a simple case of just breaking and entering. I think we're up against some very powerful criminals.'

CHAPTER NINE

Notes in the Night

I lay tucked up in my himation, my head too full of thoughts to let me go to sleep. Thrax had told me he'd worked out what the thief had taken from the secret vault but he refused to elaborate further. Which was typical of him. And that last statement on our way home had increased my curiosity. How had he figured out that the crime was committed by 'some very powerful criminals', as he called them, and not by some run-of-the-mill hoodlum in desperate need of funds?

I myself had only seen one clue in the vault. The messy handprint in the sarcophagus. It proved that the stolen object had been inside it. But as to what it could have been I had no idea, nor could I begin to guess who had stolen it. I racked my brain trying to think what you might keep in a miniature sarcophagus, besides a tortoise mummy.

'No, Nico, it was not a mummy the thief stole,' Thrax had giggled when I suggested the idea as we got ready for bed. 'The sarcophagus had been adapted into a trinket box.'

Hmm, the information was getting more intriguing by the moment. Why would someone keep a trinket box in front of an image of a god? As a sacrifice, perhaps?

'So it was a trinket of some kind?' I said.

The only answer I got was a soft snore. Thrax had fallen asleep under his himation. Bother, I would have to figure this out on my own. I opened my wax tablet to make notes. Writing always helps me sort out my jumbled thoughts and I could use the notes later for my stories. I scratched in the soft wax with the stylus.

THE CASE OF THE STOLEN LAPDOG [working title]

Crime: Melitan dog stolen from owner

Motive: To stop dog from barking and alerting witnesses to a second, more serious crime.

Second crime: Something stolen from a sarcophagus, hidden in a secret vault.

Motive of second crime: Unknown but obviously something terribly important, committed by powerful criminals.

Perpetrator: Man (or woman) who left a dirty handprint in the sarcophagus.

Clue (or clues) to identify the stolen object: Unknown.

Eventually I fell asleep with the tablet balanced on my tummy. When I woke up in the morning, sending the tablet and the stylus clattering across the floor, Thrax was already up and away. Master Ariston had sent him out to chop olive wood for the brazier.

I was also kept busy all morning and there was no opportunity to discuss the case further. Surprisingly, Master Ariston's poems had proved very popular with the guests at his father's symposium and he wanted to write some more. He would hand them out at the various celebrations during the Anthesteria.

By lunchtime, I had a pain in my thumb from holding the stylus too long so I was glad when Master Ariston stopped to eat. 'Get Cook to send me some porridge,' he said. 'I'll take it in my room. And tell Thrax to go and get me a bunch of narcissi from the market. They're for my mother. I'm dining with her tonight.'

I found Thrax sitting at the kitchen table. He was knocking seeds out of a pomegranate with Cook's wooden stirring stick.

'Ha, that's lucky,' he exclaimed when I gave him Master Ariston's instructions.

'What's lucky?' I said.

'My having to go to the market for Master Ariston. I need to run a few errands of my own. And also us two not having to work tonight. I've got plans.'

'Oooh,' I said, helping myself to lentil stew. 'What plans?'

Thrax moved his chair closer. 'I didn't spend all morning chopping wood, Nico. In fact, I didn't chop any wood at all. I borrowed some from the house next door. They have a big pile right outside their back door.'

I looked around the table in alarm, praying no one had heard him. Stealing firewood is a crime. It can land you with a hefty fine, often double the price of what you stole. The punishment would be even harsher for an unfortunate slave like Thrax. He might end up in prison, or even beaten to death.

'Don't worry,' said Thrax. 'No one noticed. And I'll replace it when I chop my own wood this afternoon.'

'So what did you do while you were meant to be chopping wood?' I asked.

'I went to see Zeno to tell him we're very close to finding out why Argos was stolen. I said it in a very loud voice to make sure everyone in the house heard me. I think it's stirred the hornet's nest. If my hunch is right, we'll see the effects of my little conversation with him tonight.'

'I'm not following,' I said.

'I'll explain later,' he said, flicking pomegranate seeds into his mouth. 'I'd better get to the market before they run out of narcissi. See you tonight, Nico, at the secret meeting place. Dig out some epiblemas, the more tattered the better. I think there are some in the storeroom.'

CHAPTER TEN

Trailing Suspects

Tattered epiblemas? Why did we need girls' shawls? Were they a part of Thrax's plan for tonight?

'Nico,' groaned Master Ariston, 'you've spilled ink all over the papyrus again. Please don't spoil any more parchment or I'll deduct the cost from your wages.'

I'd be the first to admit that I can often be clumsy but that's not why the kalamos kept slipping from my hand that afternoon. There were so many thoughts going round in my head, I just couldn't concentrate on my work.

After what seemed like an eternity trapped on the banks of the Styx, Master Ariston yawned hungrily. A delicious smell of stewed hare was wafting out of the kitchen across the courtyard. 'Let's call it a night, Nico. I have to get ready for dinner with Mother. Get my best chiton ready, the purple one with the key pattern around the border. My mother likes that one. She gave it to me last year to wear at the festival of Athena. And find Thrax. I need him to fill my bath and scrape my back.'

* * *

The moon had risen by the time Thrax and I met at the secret meeting place. He'd brought a large bag with him.

'Did you get that at the market?'

'Yes. Off a friend.'

'One of your special friends?'

'That's right.'

'Akademus?'

'No, another one. He never tells me his name. Did you find the epiblemas?'

'I did.'

'Good.' Thrax opened the bag and pulled out two old, loose-flowing chitons. They were so tattered I doubt the slaves in our house would use them as floorcloths. 'Put one of these on,' he said, 'and drape an epiblema over your shoulder.'

'We're stepping out disguised as girls?' I said.

'Best idea to prevent anyone from Zeno's household recognising us.' Thrax pulled two more things out of the bag. For one horrific moment I thought they were dead hares. But they turned out to be wigs.

'Don't tell me. You got these off one of your friends too.'

Thrax laughed. 'My friends can get hold of literally anything, as long as you don't mind the stench.'

He was right. The wigs smelled awful.

'Where did your friend get them?' I asked. 'A grave?'

'He probably raided an actor's dressing-up chest,' giggled Thrax, planting one of the wigs on my head. 'Actors are the only people I can think of who wear wigs. Although you might be right. They might have dug up an Egyptian woman's grave. I believe there are a few Egyptian people buried outside Athens.'

The thought that I might be wearing a dead person's wig was enough to make me break out in a sweat. But I didn't have time to panic. Thrax and I had to get on with our investigation. 'How do I look?' I said, straightening the wig.

'Like a dead bride come to seek her husband at the Anthesteria,' joked Thrax. He produced a lekanis.

'Oh no,' I said. 'I'm not putting on make-up.'

'It's only face powder. We have to look the part, Nico.'

By the time we climbed out of the secret meeting place and made our way to the street, I was sure we looked frightening enough to scare away the dead. It was a good job we were close to the Anthesteria. If anyone we knew spotted us, we could always claim we were on our way to a party.

'Where are we going, by the way?' I asked Thrax.

'To Zeno's house again. To observe from across the street. The more I think about it, the more I'm certain the thief had help getting into the house. Someone let him in. One of the slaves there is involved.'

'What makes you think that? I thought the thief got in through the chicken coop.'

'The hole is too small for anyone but a child of our age or less. And I don't think the thief would risk having a child crawling in and opening the back door for him. The possibility of alarming the quails and the squawking hens would be too great. They would wake up Eirene.

'Perhaps the thief himself was incredibly slim,' I suggested.

Thrax shook his head, making his wig jiggle. 'The handprint in the sarcophagus shows he was quite a beefy man. I'm hoping that what I told Zeno this morning, about us being on to the thief,

will panic the slave who was involved. He'll try to get in touch with the thief and warn him.'

'And if we follow the slave, he might lead us to him,' I said. 'Is that what you're hoping for?'

Thrax nodded. We came to the Street of the Four Winds and he started towards the back alley.

'We should watch the front of the house,' I said. 'It's coming up to the Anthesteria when masters treat their slaves as equals and let them use the front door. It would look suspicious if the guilty slave was seen creeping out of the back door, don't you think?'

We pitched up in a doorway across from Zeno's house. The house behind it seemed abandoned. The paint on the front door was blistered and the altar near it dusty and full of dead flowers.

'The perfect spot for a couple of beggars,' said Thrax.

Despite the late hour, the Street of the Four Winds was heaving with people coming in and out of houses. The spirit of the Anthesteria seemed to have gripped Athens already. Thrax placed the empty lekanis on the ground to help set the scene. I put in a handful of chalkoi for added effect.

We'd only been settled in the doorway a few moments when we heard a loud clink and another coin landed in the lekanis. A generous passer-by had thrown in an obol, enough money to buy a fresh loaf of bread or a cup of good wine. A moment later the front door across the street opened and a young man stepped out.

'That's Olympos,' said Thrax from under his epiblema.

From what I could see, Zeno's slave was very slim with wide shoulders and a chin that stuck out. He stopped for a moment to touch the feet of the Hermes statue by the front door, then sauntered away, whistling cheerfully.

'He's in a good mood,' I said. 'Not what you'd expect from a worried slave on his way to warn his partner in crime. Are we going to follow him?'

'No,' said Thrax. 'He's only going to the wine shop at the end of the street. Notice he's not wearing a himation. He doesn't mean to stay out long, and he's carrying an empty pelike. He'll be back in a moment.'

I hadn't noticed the wine shop – these places are very often just front rooms in ordinary houses – but Thrax was right. Olympos returned a few moments later, holding the pelike balanced on his right shoulder. He was still whistling cheerfully.

The front door closed behind him with a bang. A delicious smell of fried tiganites wafted out of a nearby window. My tummy growled loudly.

Suddenly the front door to Zeno's house swung open again. This time Eirene came out. She closed the door gently and looked up and down the street before hurrying off.

Thrax picked up the lekanis and we followed her at a distance. She came to the end of the street, hesitated for a moment to let a cart trundle past, then turned on to a wider road. She stopped when she came to a house next to a small temple dedicated to Hera. Thrax and I watched from a doorway as Eirene rapped on the door and was immediately let in. She didn't stay inside long.

A few moments later she came out with a child, a girl of perhaps five or six. The two of them crossed the street and sat under a statue of the goddess.

Eirene unwrapped a large honey cake and the two shared it, scattering crumbs for the doves that gathered around them. The sound of the girl's laughter carried across the street and I wondered who she was.

Before long the cake was eaten. Eirene and the girl stood up and the cook knocked on the door to the temple house again. A priestess in a flowing chiton answered it and took the child back inside.

'Well, Eirene didn't creep out to warn someone, either,' I said as we followed her back to Zeno's house.

'You're right,' Thrax agreed. 'She's not a suspect at the moment, although what we saw back there was a very important clue.'

I looked at him, puzzled. 'Was it?'

'Definitely. The whole picture is emerging very fast.'

CHAPTER ELEVEN

A Game of Petteia

We stationed ourselves in the disused doorway again. I was trying very hard to understand how Eirene sharing a honey cake with an unknown girl made the mystery clearer. To me it complicated matters. Though at least we seemed to be eliminating suspects at a quick rate.

'The thief's accomplice probably wasn't Olympos,' I said.

Thrax adjusted his wig. 'And we can eliminate Eirene and the slave Deborah. Zeno told me she's still away.'

'That leaves Hilarion,' I said. 'Though how or why an old slave would want to help a thief rob his own master, I have no idea. He looks like a decent person to me.'

Another coin clinked in the lekanis. The door to Zeno's house opened again and a stooped figure in a flowing himation stepped out. There was no mistaking Hilarion. He stood in the doorway for a moment, waved goodbye to someone inside and closed the door with a loud bang. He certainly wasn't trying to creep out unnoticed.

'Come on, Nico,' hissed Thrax. He picked up the lekanis and we followed Hilarion as he sauntered down the street. A group of children who'd been playing hide-and-seek came out of their hiding places and crowded round him.

'Got any honey cakes today, old man?'

Hilarion grinned and pulled a small package from inside his himation. The children watched in silence while he peeled back the cloth to reveal a handful of cakes.

'Me first! Me first!' They burst into a chorus of chatter as Hilarion handed out the cakes. 'Say thank you to the nice lady for us, sir. A very big thank you. She's very kind.'

Hilarion laughed. 'Don't stay out too late now. You all have to get up early for work tomorrow.'

He tucked the empty cloth back inside his himation and walked on. Thrax and I followed him out of the Kerameikos and to the agora where the stalls in the southern stoa were still doing a brisk business. Here the old slave stopped at a stall that sold cheap perfume, where he handed the stallholder an alabastron.

'The usual, Hilarion?' she asked, obviously pleased to see him.

Hilarion rummaged in his bag for a purse as the woman filled the alabastron from a jug. No more holding coins in the mouth for him, I thought, and after his frightening experience, who could blame him? Now the old slave led us past the Mint House and out on to a narrow street tucked under the walls of the Acropolis. The houses here looked old and weather-beaten. Many of them had piles of rubbish outside the front door and there was a stench of cheap wine and stale pee in the air. The noise of people roaring, laughing or fighting was deafening. A group of sailors and young women in brightly coloured garlands were dancing along the street in a long, wavy line, clinging on to each other's waists.

'What is this place?' asked Thrax.

'It's where poor people come for their fun and games,' I answered. 'Although you might spot the occasional wealthy man or famous person if you look. I hear Socrates is known to frequent the establishments on this street. He says he comes to learn all about life from the common man, but I think it's for the cheap wine.'

Hilarion stopped outside a door and rapped on it with his knuckles. It opened and he was let in.

'Should we wait for him to come out?' I asked Thrax.

'We didn't follow him all the way here to stand outside in the cold,' replied Thrax. 'We're going in too. Follow me, Nico, and don't say a word. Just smile shyly at people and nod. But don't look them in the eye. We don't want anyone finding out we're not really girls.'

We marched up to the door and Thrax knocked on it loudly. It opened again, revealing a man with a very shiny bald head. He glared at us.

'No children allowed in here,' he barked. 'Go home to bed, girls.'

The poor man seemed to have only one tooth in his mouth and his lips were swollen, as if someone had recently punched him in the mouth.

'We're desperate for some loose change, sir,' pleaded Thrax, trying to soften his voice.

The man continued to glare. 'You heard me. No children allowed. By order of the management. If you need food or money, go three doors down. It's a charity house. There are some lovely priestesses there who will give you a nice bit of bread and cheese and a bed for the night.'

Thrax rattled the coins in the lekanis. 'Let us in, sir, please. We'll be very careful not to let the owner see us begging. And we'll share our earnings with you.'

The promise of some extra money seemed to work wonders on the doorman. 'All right, come in. I suppose there's no harm in asking the men for a few chalkoi. It's nearly the Anthesteria and they might be feeling generous. But you can only stay for a short while. And don't make nuisances of yourselves or I'll chase you out.'

He opened the door a little wider and we slipped past him into an airless corridor, dimly lit with lamps hanging from the ceiling. It opened out on to a large room where wine was being served from a row of kraters by the wall. This was a kapeleion, one of Athens' infamous taverns. I was surprised that a nice man like Hilarion would even dream of coming to a place like this – unless, of course, Thrax was right and he was meeting up with a criminal. We couldn't see him in the wine room, so we stepped through a second doorway into a courtyard. Here a small group of men stood rapt in a tight circle. I heard the rattle of sharpened claws on stone and the squawk of angry birds. A cockfight was in progress. Two ruffled roosters were circling each other. Behind them stood a table with a large purse on it, the prize for the owner of the winning bird. I shuddered even to look at it. Although I relish meat after a sacrifice or at a symposium, I can't abide cruelty to animals.

'Can you see Hilarion?' I asked Thrax.

'He's not here either,' he answered, looking round the circle.

We spotted yet another doorway which had a flimsy curtain across it. Thrax pushed it aside and we entered a crowded room where men sat hunched over small tables. A woman with heavy make-up and dark hair piled high on her head was playing a lyre and singing in a rather toneless voice. No one paid her any attention. All the men in the room were concentrating on long rows of black and white pebbles in front of them. They were playing petteia, perhaps the most popular game in the Hellenic world.

Thrax pulled me towards an empty table where someone had left a half-finished game. 'Let's pretend we're playing.' We sat down and I rearranged the pebbles, lining the white ones in front of Thrax and the black ones on my side of the board.

A moment later, Hilarion came in, hastily tightening the cord around his chiton. He'd obviously been to the rest room. We kept our heads low as the old man looked around and chose a table on the other side of the room. A man in a filthy apron brought him a cup of wine from behind a counter.

Hilarion lined up the pebbles on the board. After a while another customer came in. He too looked around, then joined Hilarion at the table. He was a short man, with a light brown beard and bushy eyebrows. Not a single word passed between the two men after an initial 'khaire'. The two of them merely played, moving the pebbles across the board.

The man behind the counter brought a second cup of wine for the newcomer, who passed him some coins without looking up. The game continued.

In the courtyard, a loud roar announced the end of the cockfight. There was cheering, followed by the sounds of punching. The cockfight had

mutated into a fist fight. No one in our room seemed in the least bit alarmed. Then the curtain at the door was pushed aside again and two elderly men stepped into the room. One of them was Socrates.

My heart almost jumped into my mouth. 'Don't panic,' hissed Thrax. 'We're leaving in a moment. And Socrates won't even recognise us in these filthy wigs. Be ready to run when I tell you.'

Thrax crept up to Hilarion's table and suddenly started shaking the lekanis in the second man's face. 'A chalkoi for a hungry girl, sir. Pity a poor starving girl with no family.'

The man with the light brown beard looked up from his game with fury in his eyes. He was obviously not pleased Thrax had interrupted his game.

'Oi, you,' called the man behind the wine counter. 'No begging in here, and no children. Get out.'

'Run,' hissed Thrax, and I sprinted after him out of the room and through the courtyard. Thrax tossed the coins from the lekanis at the doorman as we burst through the front door.

'I think we were wasting our time in there,' I said as we hurried through the crowds back home. 'Hilarion was just playing a round of petteia.'

'On the contrary,' said Thrax. 'He managed to pass a message to his friend the flower-picker without saying a word except 'khaire'. A very clever set-up indeed.'

I mopped the sweat from my brow. 'Did you say the man Hilarion met is a flower-picker?' I said, whipping off my wig. 'I thought he was meeting the thief.'

'That was what I originally believed,' replied Thrax. 'But when I looked at the petteia board I saw a carefully folded note,' said Thrax. 'It was tied to one of the pebbles. Hilarion was pushing it across the board when I approached the table.'

'You mean Hilarion can write?'

'Yes,' said Thrax. 'He must have taught himself like me. I saw him writing on an old tablet when I visited Master Zeno.'

'But how do you know the man he met is a flower-picker and not the thief? That the note wasn't meant for him?'

'I don't think the man can read,' replied Thrax. 'And his hands were deeply stained with pollen, which told me he is a flower-picker. But they aren't the hands that left the print in the turtle sarcophagus. They're too small. So the flower-picker definitely isn't the thief. He's just a go-between, for the man Hilarion was trying to warn. For some reason he daren't show his face in Athens. He is still eluding us but, believe me, I will find him.'

CHAPTER TWELVE

Roasted Octopus and Fish Sauce

As we trudged home, Thrax narrowed his eyes and looked down at the ground. It was a gesture I had grown used to over the course of our investigations. I knew it meant he was sorting out clues in his head and didn't want any interruptions.

As we passed the agora, I smelled the delicious aroma of fried fish.

'Thrax,' I said, 'I don't want to intrude on your thoughts but I'm hungry. Would you like a snack too?'

He shook his head, still not saying a word, so I bought myself an enormous slice of roasted octopus in flatbread. It was dripping with fish sauce and quite delicious.

Also quite lethal, as I was soon to find out. I woke up in the middle of the night squirming with pain.

'I feel like the monster Charybdis herself is chewing away at my stomach,' I groaned when Thrax came over to see what the matter was. Sweat was running down my face and into my eyes. My skin felt clammy and despite my warm himation I shivered. 'It must have been the octopus. It was off but I couldn't tell because of the fish sauce. I'm never going to touch octopus again. Ever!'

Thrax fetched a wet rag and mopped my brow. The water felt cool on my forehead and the pain lessened a fraction.

'Try not to think about the discomfort,' said Thrax, getting back into his cot. 'Sleep if it's possible. You'll feel better in the morning. Do you want me to leave the lamp on?'

'No, thanks. Put it out. You need some rest too.'

I lay in the dark, trying to stop my teeth from chattering. My stomach rumbled like a volcano about to erupt. To take my mind off the pain, I tried concentrating on the mystery we were trying to solve. There were so many unanswered questions.

What had the thief stolen from the secret vault?

Why had Hilarion helped him? He seemed like a trustworthy man to me, not the sort that would betray his master and get involved with criminals and low-lifes.

What was the mysterious note that Hilarion had passed on to the other man?

If the flower-picker was only a go-between, who was the real thief? And why couldn't he show his face in Athens?

Towards dawn I still had none of the answers and my stomach now felt like someone had filled it with wet sand. My throat was dry, as if I'd been walking in extreme heat. Thrax was still asleep, so I tried getting out of my cot to fetch some water. Big mistake. My legs buckled under me and I crashed to the floor.

Somehow I managed to crawl back under my himation. How I wished some of the other members of the Medusa League were in Athens. Not just to help Thrax and me with the new mystery at hand, but to give me comfort in my hour of need. There's nothing like the smile of a close friend when you're ill.

Despite the heaving in my stomach, I must have drifted off to sleep because the next thing I knew, Thrax was shaking me gently.

'Nico, wake up. There's someone here to see you.'

I forced my eyes open to see the gods had granted my wish. Fotini and Gaia were standing on either side of my cot. 'Are you really here?' I asked. 'Or are you just appearing to me, like shades at the Anthesteria?'

'We're really here,' laughed Fotini, sitting down on a stool and feeling my damp brow. 'Thrax tells me you might have eaten some bad food.'

Fotini hadn't changed a bit since last summer. Tall, brimming with confidence and aware of her power, her dark eyes seemed to flash when she talked, hypnotising you. She had rescued Thrax and me from the clutches of deadly pirates on our last adventure, and I thanked the gods she was my friend.

'I'm feeling much better,' I said, 'though I doubt I can walk.'

'You must rest,' insisted Gaia, sitting gently on the edge of the cot. 'I will look after you.' She had grown taller since the summer and there seemed to be a new sparkle in her eyes. Maybe Fotini's confidence was rubbing off on her.

'My tutor in Corinth has sent me to Athens to observe the Anthesteria,' said Fotini. 'I am lodging with the priestesses of Athena. But there's no room for Gaia at the temple, so she's staying here with Master Ariston's mother and her slaves.'

'You've come at the right time,' I whispered, sitting up in my cot.

I've told them about the mystery already,' said Thrax hastily. 'You'd better rest now, Nico.'

'Thrax is right,' said Fotini. 'You must rest. We'll come and see you again this afternoon.'

Mater Ariston marched into the room moments after they'd left. He stayed well away from my cot, as if scared he might catch my sickness. 'You must have offended the gods in some way,' he snorted, 'and this is their just punishment. I hope they forgive you and you recover quickly. Meanwhile, I shall have to hire a temporary scribe. I'll pay him out of your wages.'

'Oh, but I'll be as right as rain by tomorrow, sir,' I spluttered. 'No need to hire a replacement.'

Master Ariston's mouth curled into a sneer. 'My father had this sickness once, after he'd eaten snails. It lasted for days. One minute he'd think he was over it and the next he'd be shaking with fever. I expect yours will take the same path. No, I shall definitely need a temporary scribe.'

I tried writing some notes in my tablet when Master Ariston left but, though it pains me to say it, his prediction proved to be accurate. I was soon feeling hot again and my face and arms dripped with sweat. This was followed by another chill that made my teeth chatter again. More than once I had to crawl over to the chamber pot in the corner. I was exhausted by the time Thrax came to see me early in the afternoon. He pressed a cup into my hands.

'It's a herbal potion to help settle your stomach,' he said. 'Fotini showed me how to make it. How are you feeling?'

'I think I'm getting better,' I said, 'although I think you're going to have to empty the chamber pot. It's stinking out the room.'

Thrax went out with the amis while I sipped reluctantly on the potion. It tasted horrible and, for the first time in my life, I wasn't in the mood for eating or drinking.

'I went to see Eirene the cook,' Thrax said when he returned. 'I wanted to check something.'

'Check what? Did you ask her who the little girl from the temple house was?'

Thrax opened his mouth to speak but I didn't hear the answer. Just then a stab of pain went through me like a knife. I gasped, dropped the half-empty cup and passed out.

Later I was to learn that a fever took hold of me and I lay squirming and only half conscious on my damp cot for days. The delirium brought with it strange dreams and nightmares in which I battled fierce and terrifying monsters, including the octopus I had so merrily eaten before my sickness. It wrapped its tentacles around my shoulder and laughed, releasing a cloud of foul-smelling ink. In other nightmares, I fled from criminals with pollen-yellow hands and, in the most vivid one, I saw a strange figure creeping through the door into the room...

'Have you the coins for the ferry? I am Charon, the ferryman. It is your time to cross into Hades...'

I wanted to scream and tell him to go away, to let me be. I was too young to die, surely. But my throat was dry as desert sand. So I kicked out with my legs instead. And then I felt gentle hands on my arms.

'Nico, you are awake.'

It was Gaia.

'How long have I been asleep?'

'Three days. Oh, Nico, I'm so glad you've woken up at last. I'm afraid I have some bad news to tell you. Thrax has gone missing.'

CHAPTER THIRTEEN

For Your Eyes Only

Thrax missing? I struggled to sit up in my cot. 'A boy who sells snails at the market came to tell us,' said Gaia. 'He's a friend of Thrax.'

'Thrax has many friends at the market,' I said. 'Did this one tell you his name?' It was a silly question to ask, but my mind was reeling.

Gaia shook her head. 'No he didn't and I forgot to ask. The boy said he was looking for snails in the scrub outside the Dipylon Gate when he came across Thrax hiding behind a bush.

He thinks Thrax was shadowing someone and had sprung into the hiding place when he heard him coming.'

'What made him think that?' I asked.

'The boy was about to call out a greeting when Thrax raised a finger to his lips and stopped him. The boy hurried on without saying a word but on his way back home, he found Thrax's himation caught in the bush. Oh, Nico, it had been ripped to shreds by a lion.'

'How did he know the himation was definitely Thrax's?'

'I'm not sure,' replied Gaia. 'Perhaps he recognised it. The boy brought it here and Master Ariston identified it.'

I swung my legs over the side of the cot and stood up slowly to put on my chiton. 'Have the police been informed?'

'Yes, but it seems they are too busy with other crimes to look for the remains of a slave. Apparently two other people have been killed by a lion outside Athens recently – they were guards who looked after the Acharnian Gate. Mistress said their cloaks were found ripped to shreds out-side the gate.'

'How long has Thrax been missing?' I asked.

'Two days,' said Gaia. She started sobbing. 'Oh, Nico, what are we going to do?'

I put my arm around Gaia to console her. 'Don't cry. I know Thrax very well, and I can assure you he's a match for any lion. I don't know why, but I have a feeling that he is not really dead. I think something else has happened to him and it's got to do with the mystery we're trying to solve. We need to find out what.'

Gaia looked at me with sudden hope in her eyes. 'Do you think so? Shall I tell Master Ariston? He's been crying ever since we got the news. He's even chopped off some of his hair to show he's in mourning.'

It was suprising to hear that Master Ariston had feelings for anyone else but himself, but I didn't want Gaia to put him out of his misery just yet.

'Let's not tell anyone for now,' I said. 'First we need to get in touch with Fotini. She'll help us look for him.'

'We cannot reach Fotini at the moment,' replied Gaia. 'The priestesses of Athena lock themselves away for the Anthesteria.'

'Then it'll have to be just you and me,' I said, surprising myself at how strong and decisive I sounded. 'The Medusa League to the rescue ...'

Sadly, I only managed to take a few wobbly steps across the room before I crashed to the floor. My stomach was feeling better, my head was clearer but my legs were still as weak as a newly born gosling's. Gaia helped me back to my cot before going off to do her chores.

I lay on my himation, thinking, till it got dark. By now my legs felt stronger. I crept out to the yard, ignoring the delicious scents wafting out of the kitchen. I placed my best stylus on the household altar as a sacrifice. 'Please, Mother Hera,' I begged, 'help me bring Thrax safely home. I know I sounded confident we'd find him in front of Gaia, but in truth I'm scared. You must help me ...'

There was a knock at the front door even as I stood at the altar. Herakles did not answer it. It was supper time and I guessed he was eating in the kitchen. I answered it instead. A boy stood outside. He couldn't have been more than nine but he was already muscled, and he was covered from head to toe in dust.

'Is this the house of Lykos the retired sea captain?' he asked.

'It is,' I replied.

'I want to speak with Nico the scribe,' he said.

'You're talking to him.'

The boy looked past me into the courtyard. 'Are you alone?'

'Yes,' I said. 'No one can hear us.'

'I have a message for you,' said the boy, 'from your friend Thrax.'

'From Thrax?' I stifled a gasp. 'Have you seen him? Are you one of his friends from the agora?'

'We're all friends with Thrax down at the agora,' grinned the boy. 'And he didn't pass the message on to me himself, no. He passed it to a friend, who passed it on to another friend, who passed it on to me. So I can't say as I've seen him with my own eyes. But he's sent you a note.'

He reached under his belt and pulled out a scrap of folded papyrus, which he thrust into my hands.

'Thrax said it's for your eyes only. And that's all I know.' He waited on the doorstep, whistling under his breath, until I pulled a coin out of my purse. 'Thank you, Nico,' he said. 'Enjoy the Anthesteria.'

The Anthesteria. The great festival started the day after tomorrow. I'd planned to share the fun with Thrax. Would I find him in time?

'You enjoy the Anthesteria too,' I called out after the boy. He turned and made a ghoulish face at me, crossing his eyes.

'Don't let the shades get you,' he laughed.

I closed the door, noticing that Herakles had daubed the usual patch of tar on it to keep the ghosts from entering the house. Back in my room, I sat close to the lamp and carefully unfolded the scrap of papyrus.

To my great astonishment, there was no writing in it, just a fingerprint made with golden-coloured pollen.

CHAPTER FOURTEEN

A Spot of
Tell-Tale Pollen

Gaia and I stared at the scrap of papyrus. I had called an urgent meeting of the Medusa League and, with Thrax missing and Fotini locked up in the temple, Gaia was the only member available. We sat in the secret meeting place, clutching our medallions.

It was late morning. Gaia had finished her chores in the gynaikon and Master Ariston had decided I was still too weak to go back to work. That was fine by me. Even though I was worried about my wages, I wanted to concentrate on finding Thrax.

'I stared at this fingerprint all night,' I said, 'but I can't for the life of me think what it means. Why didn't Thrax write a proper note?'

'Perhaps he didn't have time, or a pen,' suggested Gaia. 'Or he might not have wanted to run the risk of anyone reading it. He sent a message only YOU would understand.'

'Except that I don't understand it at all,' I groaned, scratching my head, then reaching for some dried fruit to help me think.

'Pollen is found in flowers,' said Gaia. 'So perhaps Thrax is telling you to think about flowers. Try to remember. Have they featured in this mystery at all?'

'Not really,' I said. 'Except we shadowed Hilarion the other day and he met up with a man who picks flowers for a living.'

'Then there's your connection,' said Gaia, sounding as decisive as Fotini. 'Isn't it obvious? We need to find this man. Chances are he might lead us to Thrax.'

'But of course!' The more I thought about it, the more I agreed with Gaia, and the more excited I felt. 'We could look for the flower-picker at the market,' I said. 'We'd have to go tomorrow, early in the morning. That's when the flower-pickers deliver their goods.'

*   *   *

It was still dark when Gaia and I met in the yard the next morning. Everyone in the house was still asleep except for Cook, who was making breakfast tiganites in the kitchen. The smell of frying pancakes and toasting pine nuts made me drool, even so soon after my sickness, but I knew we didn't have time for breakfast. We couldn't risk missing the flower-picker.

I find markets very exciting places. I love the noise, the smells, the exotic goods imported from so many different countries. But for me the most magical spot in the market is the flower section, especially at dawn when the deliveries arrive. I've been to the market at this time of day in various cities and the unfolding scene has never failed to excite me. It's like theatre.

One moment the stalls are bare, the enormous reed baskets empty and waiting. The stallholders stand about rubbing their hands to keep warm or chewing on bread and cheese for breakfast. Then the delivery men and women arrive in a blast of early-morning cheer, the flower-sellers leap into action and a frenzy of activity ensues. Before you know it, the stalls are a riot of colour and heady perfume.

'Late snowdrops from the hills. Hyacinths going cheap. Early lilies from the deepest valleys in Attica.'

Even before the flowers are in their baskets, the traders start calling out to early shoppers, mostly slaves with shopping lists made out by their masters. Only the rich can afford to buy flowers from the market. The rest pick their own.

As Gaia and I approached the agora, I could sense a great excitement in the air and, despite my sickness and the fact that Thrax was missing, I couldn't help getting caught up in the festival atmosphere. Trade is especially brisk at the market during the Anthesteria. The slaves are eager to buy the best produce for the festival. After all, they are to share in the meal at their master's table, and they are determined to sample the best food and drink possible.

The stallholders had shown their gratitude to Dionysus, the patron god of the festival, by decorating their stalls with flowers. Did I say that the Anthesteria is also a festival of flowers? People decorate their entire houses with them. They wrap miniature garlands round their drinking cups and the heads of children over the age of three.

Even though the sun had barely risen, Gaia and I had to fight our way through tight crowds of shoppers. By the time we got to the flower market, we were both out of breath and sweaty. Stallholders kept calling to Gaia and holding out small posies. 'Have this on me, little one. Get your mistress in the mood for the Anthesteria.'

Gaia had just accepted a posy of scented rosebuds when I spotted the flower-picker pushing his way through the throng. I recognised him instantly because of his unusually light brown hair and beard. He passed quite close to us and I was surprised to learn why his hair had such an unfamiliar colour. It was covered in pollen.

We followed, assured that he couldn't see us behind the enormous wicker basket on his back, which was full to the brim with scented narcissi. He stopped at a stall close to a fountain with a statue of a winged Cupid at the top.

'Good morning, Zeus,' the stallholder greeted him.

'Good morning,' replied Zeus. He unstrapped the large basket and set it gently on the ground. 'It was freezing out in the hills today but I got enough narcissi to last you through the three days of the Anthesteria.'

'Good man,' said the stallholder. 'Put them over here in a heap. I'll sort them out as soon as I have a spare moment.' He took some coins out of a large purse and paid Zeus. The flower-picker thrust them under his belt and set off, his now-empty basket jiggling on his back.

Gaia and I followed him, pushing our way through the crowds. He stopped at a food stall for his breakfast, which he ate with the empty flower basket still strapped to his back. Once finished, he left the agora, walking past a small temple with an altar dedicated to the twelve gods. Outside the market, the streets were quiet and empty. The only sound was the birdsong in the trees and the splashing of fountains. Gaia and I hurried along, taking care to leave a discreet distance between us and the flower-picker.

Once we nearly got splashed when a woman emptied her chamber pot out of an upstairs window. A dog barked ferociously as we passed a door painted all over with nymphs. Zeus didn't even look back. He hurried on, leading us away from the centre of Athens to a district in the south-west called Koele. The streets here were narrower than the ones in our part of the city, the houses smaller and shabbier. Children were already playing in the dust and women sang as they cooked. No hiding in a gynaikon for these busy mothers with children to look after and mouths to feed. Lacking space for a kitchen inside, they cooked outside their front doors. Zeus stopped at a house with a green door, removed the flower basket from his back and went in.

'I'm home,' we heard him call out before the door closed behind him.

'What do we do now?' asked Gaia.

'We'll come back tonight,' I said. 'If he's to lead us to Thrax I'm sure it'll be at night. The streets will be full of people celebrating the Anthesteria and that'll make shadowing him easier. Come on, let's get home. You'll be in trouble if Master Lykos's wife finds out you've been out of the house without permission.'

CHAPTER FIFTEEN

In the Graveyard

Pithogia, the first night of the Anthesteria

The sun had set and Master Lykos's house echoed with the sound of music, laughter and feasting. Tonight was the first night of the Anthesteria and we all sat in the courtyard, masters next to slaves, men besides women, friends of the family mingling with relatives who had travelled to Athens especially for the festival. Only Master Ariston did not seem to be in a jolly mood. He sat in a corner, his face glum, and I knew he was missing Thrax. It was a side of my employer I had never seen before and I have to say it endeared him to me.

Herakles, assisted by two other male slaves, carried in a large pithoi and set it down carefully in front of Master Lykos.

'Behold, the new wine,' called out Master Lykos, getting to his feet. 'We thank the great Dionysus for his generosity and beg him to be kind to us in the coming months, when the sun will warm the grapes and the rain water the land.

'All hail Dionysus,' roared everyone, Gaia and I among them.

Master Lykos broke the seal on the pithoi and the first drops of wine were poured into his kylix, his drinking cup. Later he would offer some of that wine to the god at one of the household altars but now it was time for the feast. Cook, helped by some girls hired especially for the banquet, hurried out of the kitchen with dishes of stewed meat and roasted lily bulbs. Herakles and his helpers poured wine for the other guests.

Despite the merry atmosphere, none of us could forget that this was also a festival of the dead. The first two days were especially dangerous, with ghosts believed to be looking for relatives who were still living. One touch of a ghost's spectral finger and you were doomed to wander the banks of the Styx forever. The children, especially, kept glancing behind their backs, keeping a lookout for the dead. Some kept running to the front door, to touch the patch of sticky tar for good luck.

Gaia and I managed to slip out of the house halfway through the celebrations. We hurried across a city busy with people to Koele.

None of the cramped houses on Zeus's street had rooms or courtyards big enough to host festivities, so the people had come together on the street to celebrate. They'd set up tables heaving with fried food and wine jars, and the air echoed with the sound of laughter and merrymaking. I felt we were in no danger of being noticed in the crowd as we kept an eye out for Zeus.

We didn't have to wait long for him. We spotted him coming out of his door, touching the dab of black pitch for protection. He didn't have the wicker flower basket strapped to his back. Instead he carried a sack over one shoulder.

Gaia and I followed him all the way to the Dipylon Gate on the west side of the city, which had also been daubed with tar. He stopped to talk to the guards and I heard the clink of coins as money changed hands in a bribe. The gate swung open. Suddenly Gaia pulled me forward and we ran through before the guards had time to close it again.

'You're becoming very resourceful,' I said to Gaia. 'Slipping past city guards like that.' The praise made her beam.

'I don't think they even noticed us, to be honest.' She giggled. 'They were celebrating the Anthesteria too. Did you see the wine jars and the bowls of food?'

The Dipylon Gate opens on to a vast cemetery. The road that cuts through it is lined with graves. Some are marked with pottery vases half buried

in the soil. Others have a proper gravestone or stele carved with statues of the people buried underneath. Further away from the road, the graves are grander. They look like miniature temples with columns and sloping roofs. That night, even the graveyard had a festive, if gruesome, aspect to it. Many of the graves were decorated with bunches of flowers. Food and wine had been left as a sacrifice to the dead.

Ahead of us, Zeus had been walking along the main path, but soon he left it and started picking his way through the graves. The cemetery here was unkempt, the old gravestones half sunk into the earth or even smashed.

Zeus kept on walking till he came to a tomb built into a cliff. It was a huge family tomb with Doric columns on either side of a thick door. Zeus produced a large key from under his belt and the door creaked open. He disappeared inside, leaving the door ajar. Gaia and I heard muffled voices and the sounds of what I took to be a scuffle. Then Zeus came out again and slammed the door shut behind him. The key grated in the lock.

His bag now hung empty from his hand. He'd obviously left its contents inside. Had he brought food to the people whose muffled voices we'd heard? Gaia and I crouched behind a gravestone as Zeus smoothed his himation. He turned to the grave and mumbled a short prayer. He was a tough man, perhaps a ruthless criminal, but he wasn't taking any chances that the ghosts of the dead whose final resting place he'd violated might follow him. His prayer said, he hurried away without looking back.

When Gaia and I were sure he'd gone, we stepped up to the vault. I was certain the people in the tomb were being held prisoner.

'Hello,' I called. 'Can you hear us? We're friends.'

There was a sort of muffled reply on the other side of the door.

I turned to Gaia. 'How do we get in?'

'Allow me!' To my astonishment, Gaia removed the pin from her himation and proceeded to pick the lock.

'Who taught you to do that?' I said, unable to believe my eyes.

'It's a skill I learned from the priestesses at the temple in Aegina,' replied Gaia as she jiggled the pin in the lock. 'The followers of Athena must not only be sound in mind and spirit. They must also be prepared for every eventuality.'

I heard a loud squeak as the lock turned. Gaia pulled open the door and I peered in to see three people huddled at the bottom of a short flight of stairs. They had their hands and feet tied and gags across their mouths.

One of them was Thrax.

CHAPTER SIXTEEN

Centaur Alpha

I had to keep myself from bursting into tears when I saw Thrax safe and sound, and I offered a quick thank you to the gods. Gaia had reached into my bag and was now busy hacking away at his gag with my stylus sharpener.

'I knew you'd come, Nico,' he said, when the filthy piece of cloth had fallen away from his mouth. I took the stylus sharpener from Gaia and started cutting through the rope around his hands.

'The fingerprint clue had me stumped for a while,' I said. 'But Gaia helped me work out what it meant.'

'Clever Gaia,' laughed Thrax. 'We might make her leader of the Medusa League one day. I'm sorry it wasn't easy to decipher, Nico, but I couldn't run the risk of anyone finding out that I was trying to contact you. I left the note with one of my friends in the market, with strict instructions to deliver it to you should he hear something had happened to me.'

'One of your friends discovered you were in trouble,' I said. 'He found your himation caught in a bush. It had been ripped to shreds and he assumed you'd been attacked by a lion. Everyone thought you were dead. Master Ariston is inconsolable.'

'Ha,' said Thrax. 'The old goat does have feelings after all. But that was just a stupid stunt pulled by my abductors. They wanted to make sure no one would come looking for me.'

'Who really attacked you?' asked Gaia.

'The flower-picker,' replied Thrax. 'I was shadowing him and he must have suspected he was being followed because suddenly he turned round and leaped on me. I was taken completely by surprise. Good job I'd made that cryptic note.'

'I wish I'd been there to defend you,' growled Gaia fiercely, which made Thrax laugh.

With only the one stylus sharpener between us, it took Gaia and me quite a while to free Thrax and the two other prisoners. But at last we all stumbled out into the moonlight.

It was obvious from their grubby uniforms that the men were guards.

'I'm Theodorus,' said the younger one. 'And this is Simos.'

'We keep watch at the Acharnian Gate,' said Simos, rubbing his wrists where the tight rope had cut into the skin. 'We were out hunting for hares just over a week ago. Trying to catch some meat for the Anthesteria. A group of masked hoodlums attacked us and locked us up in that tomb.'

'Oh,' cried Gaia. 'My mistress said that two guards had been mauled to death by a lion. Their bodies were never found but their cloaks were discovered outside the Acharnian Gate. The kindnappers pulled the same stunt for you too.'

'We were well fed every night,' growled Simos. 'Which makes me think we were destined for a slave market in some distant country.' He held out his hand to me when we came to the main path. 'That was a narrow escape. We're indebted to you and your friends, young man. When the Anthesteria is over, we mean to talk to our superiors. We won't rest till the kidnappers are caught. Meanwhile, if ever you need anything, you can find us at the Acharnian Gate.'

We watched the guards disappear towards the city. 'I wasn't kidnapped just to be sold,' said Thrax. 'The flower picker wanted me out of the way.'

'We shadowed him ourselves and he led us to you,' I said. 'His name is Zeus, by the way.'

'I noticed he didn't turn back towards the city when he came to the main path,' said Gaia. 'He took another route, away from Athens.'

'That path leads to a sacred grove dedicated to Athena,' said Thrax. 'It is also held in high regard by... the Spartans. His hand flew to his mouth to stifle a gasp. 'Why didn't I make the connection before? Hurry up, we must get there as soon as possible.'

We trotted along the path and before long we saw the gnarled trees of the sacred grove looming up before us. They were truly ancient, their twisted branches reaching towards the sky.

'Let's be careful,' said Thrax. 'I don't want to get caught again.'

I could see flickering lights among the trees. Was someone celebrating the Anthesteria here too? If so, there was no sound of laughter or merrymaking. I could hear voices but they were raised in a mournful chant, carried on the wind.

Thrax crouched down in the long grass and crawled forward on his hands and knees. Gaia and I followed him. Among the olive trees, a group of men was sitting on stools that formed a large circle on the grass. Every one of them had the end of his himation pulled up over his head and every single cape bore the same letter in golden thread that glowed in the moonlight.

The lambda.

I'd seen that letter before – on the mosaic in Zeno's andron.

As we crouched in the grass, a man arrived on horseback. Zeus, whom we hadn't noticed before but who must have been waiting under a tree, ran forward to help him down from the saddle. Unlike the other men, the newcomer's head was bare. He had the scariest face I'd ever seen and I was chilled to the bone just looking at it. The skin was shiny and wrinkled like old parchment. One of his eyes seemed to stare blankly and I realised it was made of marble.

The man took an empty stool in the circle. He cleared his throat. 'Gentlemen, a lot of you have communicated with me many times but none of you have met me face to face until now. I have a good old-fashioned Spartan name in real life, but you can call me Centaur Alpha. For years my family has been dedicated to overthrowing Athens and establishing Sparta as the dominant force in the world. One of my ancestors set up the Secret Society of Centaurs, of which you are all members, right here in Attica under our enemies' noses.

'And why do we call ourselves centaurs? Because centaurs are noble and powerful, quick to anger and fearless. Our society was established to harness the power of all your wealth, your power, and your will to overthrow Athens.

'Well, the time to act is upon us. I sent word to Sparta and now the answer has come. Our forces are waiting, our people are prepared, our ships are poised to set sail. We have permission to strike. Tonight is the first night of that most beloved of Athenian festivals: the Anthesteria. For three days chaos and disorder will reign over the city. It's the perfect time to deal the first deadly blow. Are you ready?'

A loud cheer echoed from the men on the stools.

'Aye, we are ready.'

Centaur Alpha stood up. He seemed to be looking through the trees at something in the distance. I turned and realised what it was at once. The colossal bronze statue of Athena in the Acropolis. The tip of her helmet flashed like the morning star in the cold light of dawn.

'Offer your sacrifices to the dark gods,' bellowed Centaur Alpha. 'Call for help in our noble mission and wait for my instructions. Tomorrow night, we strike.'

CHAPTER SEVENTEEN

A Cunning Plan

Choes, the second night of the Anthesteria

'I think I shall hide in here until we work out what to do next,' said Thrax, sinking on to one of the stools in the secret meeting place.

Thrax, Gaia and I had hurried back home at dawn, wading through mounds of rubbish from the first night of the Anthesteria. Gaia had been collared to help clear up in the courtyard, but I was free to join Thrax. The temporary scribe was not due to leave till the day after the festival.

'I wonder what the centaurs meant when they swore to destroy Athens,' I said. 'There's been rumours about going to war with Sparta, of course, but they've never come to anything. And what do these men have to do with it? If they're all the same age as the one with the glass eye, they're too old for open combat. They're even too old to be generals.'

Thrax was about to reply when we heard footsteps outside the meeting place. I looked through a crack in the hollow tree trunk to see Master Ariston sauntering along with the temporary scribe. They stopped to take a rest on a stone bench very close to our tree.

'Are you looking forward to the second night of the Anthesteria?' asked Master Ariston.

'Yes,' replied the scribe. 'We don't have grand festivals like this back home.'

'Tonight will be even wilder, at least for the common people,' said Master Ariston. 'Most of them will spend the evening dressed up as the ghoulish servants of Dionysus. They will go round the city playing tricks on their friends. But a select few like us will attend a grand and secret event to which only the rich and powerful are invited. There will be a play where the chosen queen of the festival marries Dionysus himself.' He chuckled. 'A marriage made in Hades, if you like. You are very lucky to be invited.'

'It was my uncle who managed to get me an invitation, sir,' replied the scribe. 'He is well connected, even in Athens.'

'Of course,' said Master Ariston. 'He is a famous stonemason after all. You'll enjoy the evening.'

I felt a pang of jealousy at the way our master spoke to the new scribe. He talked to him as an equal rather than a servant like me. No doubt it was because he came from a rich family.

'Of course, I shan't enjoy the event much myself,' said Master Ariston. 'I just can't stop thinking about Thrax. The sight of that himation ripped to shreds has given me nightmares. A himation I bought him with my own money! And of course I won't have him attending me tonight. I shall be slave-less. Oh, the shame of it.'

He sniffed dramatically. 'Usually the secret event is performed in the grounds of the bouleuterion, the famous assembly house in the agora, but tonight it's going to be held outside the Parthenon in the Acropolis. The painters have just finished the decorations on the frieze and General Pericles wants to show them off.'

'Is the great man himself going to be there?' asked the scribe. 'I heard he never attends public festivals on account that he is worried about his looks.'

'He does turn down a lot of invitations,' agreed Master Ariston. 'He has a big, sloping forehead and I have it on good authority that he wears a helmet made especially to hide it. Not a successful experiment, I would think. It only draws attention to it.'

'Quite,' said the scribe.

'All these famous people who lack breeding are so concerned about their looks and reputations,' continued Master Ariston. 'But I'd be willing to gamble my precious lyre that Pericles will be at the Acropolis tonight. It's his project, his baby.

He's been waxing lyrical about it for years. He'll want to be there to drink in all the glory. I suppose I had better get to the barber's as soon as possible. I don't want to be seen at a public event with an untidy beard and hair. You should come too. Make yourself look handsome for the girls.'

Thrax dug me in the ribs as Master Ariston and the scribe headed back towards the house.

'Nico,' he whispered, his voice echoing around the tree trunk like some ancient oracle. 'I've just figured out how Centaur Alpha is going to strike the first blow at Athens. We need to find ourselves some masks.'

CHAPTER EIGHTEEN

Masks for the Festival

They were out of masks at the market, even in the big expensive shops inside the southern stoa. Not surprising really, seeing as everyone in Athens seemed to be wearing one.

'Why don't you go home and see if Gaia is free to help you make some yourself?' said Thrax. 'I have to meet one of my friends.'

'What's this one teaching you?' I laughed. 'Escaplogy?'

'Officially he's a purse-snatcher,' said Thrax. 'But his talents run to more than just yanking purses off belts. He...'

'That's enough, thank you,' I said in mock horror. 'I don't need to know any more. See you back at the meeting place.'

At home I found some discarded sheets of papyrus. Gaia, who'd been given some time for an afternoon nap, helped me cut out the masks, which we soaked in ink. As we hung them out to dry on our tree, we discussed the evening ahead.

'This is turning out to be quite an Anthesteria,' I said. 'Both a festival and a mystery rolled into one.'

Gaia sighed. She wasn't thinking about the festival. 'I wish we could go to the police.'

'And tell them a one-eyed Spartan who calls himself Centaur Alpha is going to start a war between Athens and Sparta? They'll just think we've been drinking wine behind our masters' backs. Besides, we have to catch Centaur Alpha doing something that will get him put away. Then he won't be able to carry out the rest of his evil plan. The centaurs will be leaderless.'

'Then I wish Fotini was coming with us,' said Gaia. 'She'll be very disappointed to miss out on an adventure.'

Thrax arrived just as we were punching thread holes in the masks. Even if I have to say it myself, the masks looked as good as any you would find at the agora. I was really proud of them.

'How are we going to get into the Acropolis?' I asked.

Thrax shrugged. 'Have you any suggestions, Nico?'

'We can't scale the walls, that's for sure. The Acropolis is really a fort designed to keep attackers out. It's built on a very steep hill. And we won't be able to sneak in at the main gate. It will be heavily guarded.' I grinned as a brilliant idea occurred to me. 'We could ask Socrates to let us in. I'm sure he's been invited.'

'That's a great idea. Let's go and see him right away.'

We hurried through the Dipylon Gate to the outer Kerameikos, a large section of the potters' district outside the city walls. Socrates lived here, along with many artists and great thinkers who believed it was fashionable to live among ordinary workers. We heard a loud crash as we knocked on his door. Socrates answered it himself.

'That was not Xanthippe,' he said, hopping up and down on one foot. 'I just dropped a krater on my toe. What can I do for you, boys?'

'We were wondering if you were attending the Anthesteria celebrations at the Acropolis tonight, sir?' asked Thrax.

'But of course,' replied Socrates. 'General Pericles is unveiling the final decorations in the Parthenon frieze. And there will be free wine, my friend, rivers of it. Why do you ask?'

'We need to be in the Acropolis during the festivities, sir.'

Socrates looked from Thrax to me. 'Is this something to do with Zeno's little mystery?'

'Yes, sir.'

'My word, I take it that your hunch was right, young man. The small, insignificant mystery leads to a bigger, more significant one.'

'It looks like it, sir.'

'I'll arrange for a trusted guard to let you in. His name is Leon.'

'How will he know you sent us, sir?' asked Thrax.

'I'll write you a note,' said Socrates. He scribbled something on a small piece of papyrus and handed it to me. 'You show him this. He'll let you in. Good luck, boys, and perhaps I'll see you there.'

'May we ask that you tell absolutely no one about our mission, sir?' said Thrax.

Socrates tapped the right side of his nose to show he understood. 'Silence is the mother of surprise, boys.'

CHAPTER NINETEEN
A Note from Socrates

Time passes awfully slowly when you're waiting, but at last it got dark. A strong breeze rattled the branches of the trees. It was a fitting sound for the spooky night that lay ahead.

Thrax, Gaia and I put on our masks, pinned on our himations and climbed out of the secret meeting place. I checked to make sure Socrates' message was safely tucked under my belt.

'We should have brought cloaks,' I said in a last-minute panic as we came on to the main street. 'All rich people have a chlamys. We can't turn up at the Acropolis without them. It'll make us look suspicious.'

'Stop worrying, Nico,' said Thrax. 'It'll be too dark for anyone to notice us once we're inside the Acropolis.'

The streets were a sea of fast-walking, elbow-pushing, loud-talking people. The whole city seemed to be on its way to visit relatives, bearing extravagant gifts of food and wine. Choes, the second night of the Anthesteria, was all about giving and sharing, about telling your loved ones how much you appreciated them.

It was also the second night of ghosts and ghouls. No one knew which faces in the crowd belonged to the dead. Look at that old woman there, hobbling along with the help of a stick. Is she dead or alive? Don't let her touch even the hem of your himation or you too might find yourself following Persephone to the underworld. Better make sure your mask was securely tied to your face. That way the dead might mistake you for one of them and leave you alone. It's a good idea to chew on some hawthorn leaves too. They say the dead shy away from its smell like cats from lavender.

We stopped to buy hawthorn from an old man. The hill of the Acropolis loomed up before us as we skirted the packed agora. I could see statues and the roofs of familiar buildings gleaming in the light of a thousand flaming torches. The highest belonged to the newly built Parthenon, said to be the most perfect temple in the world. Towering above it was the giant bronze statue of Athena I had seen from the sacred grove the night before. She held her spear at her shoulder as if preparing to throw it.

I knew that there was a second statue of Athena inside the temple. It was even richer than this one. Its clothes were made of pure gold, its face and hands carved in ivory.

No matter how many times you visit the Acropolis, you cannot help but feel a shiver of excitement as you walk up the marble steps towards the main entrance, the propylaea. You know that this is the most sacred temple complex in the world, beloved of Athena, the

patron-goddess and protector of our city. You know that no matter where you go in the world, you will never see finer art or more perfect architecture.

Even the gate itself, a mere entrance, looks like an extravagant temple made of both white and grey marble. It is actually not one but five gates. They help the guards control the flow of people in and out of the Acropolis.

Thrax, Gaia and I hurried up the marble steps, taking care not to lose each other in the heaving crowd.

'Keep a hold of your purse, Nico,' warned Thrax. 'I think there are a lot of thieves around.'

'Some of your friends?' I teased.

We approached the middle gate, making sure our masks were in place, and Thrax spoke to one of the guards.

'We're looking for one of your colleagues, Leon. We have a message for him.'

The guard sneered. 'You turn around and go back home, children. No one is allowed in the

Acropolis tonight unless they have a special invitation.'

'But we have a message for Leon,' said Thrax.

'Leon is busy. I said move on.'

Thrax and I backed away from the gate. 'What do we do now?' I asked.

'We approach another gate.'

We joined a second queue and were soon facing another guard. This one sounded a bit kinder than the first. 'You're looking for Leon?' he said. 'Hold on a moment.' He turned to a group of guards standing at ease beyond the gates. 'Is Leon there? There's two young lads and a girl who want to see him.'

A young guard with enormous feet and very hairy knees sauntered over. 'What do you want, children?'

'We have a message, sir,' said Thrax, 'from Socrates the philosopher.'

'Well, hand it over,' said the guard.

Thrax turned to me. 'Go on, Nico, give him the message.'

I reached under my belt for the papyrus. But there was nothing there. The note from Socrates was gone.

CHAPTER TWENTY

The Way in to the Acropolis

'I should have made sure it was safe,' I groaned as the three of us pushed our way through the crowds. 'It must have been stolen. Who'd steal a scrap of papyrus?'

Gaia put a comforting arm around my shoulder. 'Don't blame yourself, Nico. It could have happened to anyone.'

'But what do we do now?' We reached the bottom of the steps and a river of Anthesteria masks flowed past us. We seemed to be the only people heading away from the Acropolis.

Thrax surveyed the people around us. 'I guess we'll have to ask one of my notorious little friends for help.' He put his thumb and forefinger in his mouth and gave a piercing whistle that startled a good number of people.

Almost immediately a boy with oily hair that stood up in tufts slipped out of the crowds. He had scabby knees and a well-used sling tied around his waist like a belt. 'You called, Thrax?'

'Hello, Akademus,' said Thrax. 'Been out shooting pigeons with that sling? These are my friends, Nico and Gaia. We want to get into the Acropolis. Do you know a secret way in? It's very important.'

Akademus's eyes glowed like newly minted coins. 'My beloved friend Thrax goes in free,' he said. 'But your friends? It will cost two chalkoi each. Payable in advance.'

I paid up, feeling that at least I was doing something to correct my mistake. Maybe everything was not lost and we'd get into the

Acropolis after all. Akademus led us round to the eastern side of the hill. The rocks here were jagged and pockmarked with caves. Thrax stopped to look around the dusty landscape.

'Ha,' he said. 'I never noticed how many little caves there are under the Acropolis. And look, Nico, some of them have been turned into small shrines.'

There were very few people on this side of the hill, away from the agora and the propylaea, but we could hear the sounds of merrymaking in the distance. The sound of tympanums, krotalas and koudounias floated down from the Acropolis.

'Come on, you three. Hurry up. You're missing the entertainment,' Akademus urged as he scrambled up a rocky slope dotted with bushes. I could smell the sharp aroma of thyme and lavender and I felt my chest tighten. I was already out of breath.

Akademus stopped by a gnarled tree, waved to us with both hands and promptly disappeared. A few moments later Thrax disappeared too, and then Gaia. I hurried after them to discover there was a small cave behind the tree. It was the entrance to a tunnel.

'A natural storm drain, carved by streams a long time ago,' said Thrax. 'Come on, Nico.'

We followed Akademus, feeling the path coiling and twisting around us. It felt like we were walking inside a giant buried serpent. After a while we saw a dim light ahead and came out into a chamber cut in the rocks. A lamp burned in a niche in the wall. A few himations were lined up neatly on the floor.

'Is this where you and your friends sleep at night?' Thrax asked Akademus.

'It's one of our many homes in the city.'

'It's cosy,' I said, looking around in admiration. 'Get a few stools or cushions and it would make the perfect meeting place. You and your friends could hold secret meetings in here.'

'We do,' laughed Akademus. 'There's a whole warren of tunnels under the Acropolis. But we must go on.'

We picked our way through more dark passages, often having to bend down to avoid grazing our heads against sharp rocks. After a while we heard water gushing.

'This brook feeds the klepsydra,' said Akademus, 'a spring that has been turned into a fountain. It's in a cave almost at the foot of the Acropolis. I believe people worship a water nymph in it.'

We came to a makeshift ladder half hidden behind a curtain of ferns.

'Is this how you and your friends get into the Acropolis?' Thrax asked Akademus.

The boy grinned sheepishly. 'We sometimes use it after there's been a sacrifice to Athena. The priests leave a lot of roasted meat behind. No sense in letting the vultures have it.'

He pointed to the top of the ladder. 'You'll come up behind a small shrine. But don't let anyone see you climbing out or the priests will have the hole blocked up.'

He held the ladder while we climbed up towards a bush hiding the hole. I heard the distant sound of music. There was no time to ask Thrax what we were going to do once we got out in the Akropolis, but I had a horrible feeling our lives would soon be in mortal danger.

And I was right.

CHAPTER TWENTY ONE

Face to Face with General Pericles

I have no idea how many important citizens there are in Athens but a good many of them had been sent a coveted invitation to Pericles's special ceremony. It was impossible to recognise anyone wearing their masks, but I knew there must be a few familiar faces behind them, including Socrates and Master Ariston. And Master's temporary scribe, of course, although he is by no means an important person.

The temples of the Acropolis were so brightly lit by flaming torches that they gleamed like ice. The bronze statue of Athena glowed as if on fire. She looked serene despite the war helmet and spear.

The guests had brought the celebratory mood of the Anthesteria with them and many were tucking into delicious-smelling meals, carried in small baskets by their slaves. It seemed we had arrived only moments before General Pericles himself. Even as we tried brushing the dust from our himations, there was a loud fanfare at the gates and the general marched in with his entourage.

The mood in the Acropolis grew serious at once. Slaves put away uneaten food and flasks of wine. Pericles walked with a very firm step, a man confident of his power and ability. He too wore a mask and he did not take off his helmet as the chief priest of Dionysus came forward to welcome him.

Thrax, Gaia and I wormed our way through the crowd to get a better view. Pericles introduced the priest to Phidias, the famous sculptor who had carved the two statues of Athena. Next he introduced Mnesikles, who had designed the propylaea, and then Ictinus and Callicrates, the architects of the Parthenon.

'Welcome, all,' said the priest. 'The gods have blessed us with a double celebration tonight. Many of Athens' important citizens are getting their first glimpse of the Parthenon, and of course, it is the second night of the Anthesteria. We celebrate the wedding of the god Dionysus to the ritual queen of Athens, the wife of our consul. We opened last year's wine at the temple yesterday, General. Would you and your guests care for some?'

General Pericles had no time for wine. He was eager to start the tour of the Parthenon. The priest called out and the priestess of the temple of Athena came forward. Several men came with her, lighting her way with torches. The sound of cymbals and castenets, which had fallen silent at the arrival of the general, started up again.

The priestess led Pericles and his entourage to the magnificent temple where Phidias took over to point out the unique decorations. We managed to squeeze in with them, three almost invisible shadows at the edge of the group.

The rectangular Parthenon was surrounded by Doric columns. At the top of them ran a frieze, a series of carvings showing scenes from mythology. Here were sculptures showing the epic battles. In one, the Olympian gods fought a mythical race of superhuman hoplites called the gigantes. In another, Greek soldiers did battle with a horde of giant female warriors known as the Amazons. And yet another showed the same battle between centaurs and mortals that we had seen in Zeno's mosaics.

The sight of the beautifully carved yet gruesome centaurs reminded me of Centaur Alpha. Was he here already? I wondered. Was he mingling with the crowds, his face hidden by a mask? What did he intend to do?

Phidias led the most impoprtant guests under the portico, the space behind the columns, and the rest of us trooped behind them round the temple, like pilgrims in a procession. There was

a second frieze running along the top of them. It showed a scene from the festival of Athena, with people following a statue of the goddess from the graveyard in the outer Kerameikos and up to the Acropolis. And then we stepped inside to admire the sculptor's masterpiece.

The towering statue of Athena welcomed us with a godly stare. She was made of gold and ivory but she looked almost real in the lamplight and I felt I was standing in the presence of the goddess herself. Her eyes seemed to pierce through to my very spirit.

'She's magnificent, isn't she?' said Pericles, who was obviously not intimidated by being in the presence of the goddess. 'I think of her as a treasury on two legs! If we ever need funds for a war, gentlemen, all we have to do is melt down the gold and pawn the ivory. There's even more gold stored in the loft above us.'

This revelation sent a nervous laugh rippling through the entourage. The priest of Dionysus coughed to show his disapproval and announced the second part of the programme. We trooped outside to watch a parade. The ritual queen of Athens was led through the gate on a cart covered in garlands. She was bedecked from head to toe in flowers and accompanied by a long trail of older women, assistants who walked behind her.

The queen's real-life husband, himself a priest, appeared dressed in a leopard skin to show he was playing the part of Dionysus. He helped the queen down from the cart and led her into the temple for a secret ceremony.

Only a handful of important people were allowed to watch it but I later I heard about it from Master Ariston himself. The ceremony was really a play, with the queen of Athens and her husband re-enacting the sacred marriage between Ariadne and Dionysus. It was a ritual designed to please the god.

While we all waited outside the temple, listening to the sound of an aulos coming from inside, Thrax had been looking around, peering through his mask.

'What's the matter?' I said.

He answered in an urgent whisper. 'Stay close to me, Nico. Gaia! Something's about to happen.'

Suddenly an enormous shadow of a centaur sprang on to the columns of the Parthenon. Thrax leaped at Pericles and pulled him to the ground. A moment later a knife whizzed past the spot where the general had been standing. It buried itself in Ictinus's shoulder and I stared at the hilt in disbelief.

It was shaped like a lambda.

A moment later the crowd around me erupted like a volcano. Screaming rang in my ears and I saw everyone in Pericles's entourage make a dive towards Thrax. Only one person in the crowd seemed to be standing still. He was wearing a mask showing a ghostly face. The eyes behind it were glaring at me with pure hatred. Or I should say only *one* eye glared. The other one stared blankly. It was made of marble.

'Centaur Alpha,' I gasped.

CHAPTER TWENTY TWO

Traitors and Heroes

Centaur Alpha's eye bore into me for a moment longer, then he leaped through the panicked crowd and disappeared among the writhing storm of masks and dark himations. I tried to run after him but someone grabbed me roughly by the shoulder and practically lifted me off my feet.

'Where do you think you're going?'

I could see from the corner of my eye that it was the first guard who had turned us away from the gate.

For a brief moment after the knife had been thrown, the crowd had succumbed to hysteria. But it regrouped with frightening efficiency. A lot of the guests in the Acropolis were high-ranking military men and they barked out orders to the people around them.

'Calm down! Stop rushing around.'

Pericles got to his feet, setting his helmet straight. A guard had grabbed Thrax and was twisting his arm behind his back. One of the guests ripped the mask from his face.

'Let's see the assassin's face.'

'Don't hurt him,' begged a tremulous voice beside me. It was Gaia. She stepped forward bravely, removing her own mask. 'He's not the killer. You've got the wrong man. He was trying to SAVE General Pericles!'

The guard who had grabbed me pulled off my mask and I felt the cold breeze against my face.

'Here's another one of them. I noticed these three children crawling out of a bush near the temple of Pandroseion over by the walls. Been keeping an eye on them all night.'

'They might be children,' bellowed a man in the crowd. 'But they're also traitors. Throw them over the wall.'

As the man's words echoed around the Acropolis, the elite crowd seemed to change into a baying mob of common people. We were dragged towards the wall behind the Chalcothece, the great storehouse where all bronze offerings to Athena are kept.

'Hurl them right over,' screamed someone. 'Send them straight to the underworld.'

'Wait! Stop this madness, I implore you.' A voice I recognised startled the crowd into silence. 'Call yourself the elite? You're behaving like mad barbarians at a bull run.' The man removed his mask. It was Socrates. He approached Pericles. 'The girl is right, General. That young man is not the would-be assassin, nor is the other his accomplice. I know these children well. They are honest citizens and would never try to harm you. If they say they saved your life, I for one believe them. In my eyes, they are heroes.' He turned to Thrax. 'Did you see the real assassin?'

'Yes.'

Socrates spoke to Pericles again. 'While your men are trying to outperform Euripides' theatre company in drama and hysterics, General, I should imagine the real culprit is making good his escape, so he can try to kill you again another day.'

The philosopher put his hand on Thrax's shoulder. 'You are the only one who can bring the criminal to justice. If Pericles gives you permission, will you go after him?' He handed Thrax a jewelled dagger.

Thrax wiped the dust from his face. 'If I can borrow a horse, sir.'

'Take my own,' said the general. 'Socrates is a close friend of mine and I have no reason to doubt him. But bring him back unharmed, and bring me the assassin too. May Athena go with you.'

The sea of himations parted to let Thrax through and he sprinted down the marble steps of the propylaea.

Beside me, a tall man removed his mask. Tears were running down his face. It was Master Ariston.

'It's my precious Thrax,' he sobbed. 'He has come back from the dead. Long live Athena!'

CHAPTER TWENTY THREE

The Chase, the Capture

Thrax told me later what happened next so that my story would be complete. Even as the mob was trying to hurl us over the walls of the Acropolis, he had already spotted the assassin scrambling down the steep hill. Thrax guessed Centaur Alpha had someone waiting for him with a horse, and he knew where he would be heading too. The Dipylon Gate. It would not have been closed that night, so as to allow the citizens of

Athens to pay their respects to the dead in the Kerameikos graveyard.

Thrax thundered after Centaur Alpha on Pericles's horse, catching up with him near Market Hill outside the agora. Centaur Alpha heard the hoof beats and turned round in the saddle. He yanked the reins on his own horse so hard, the poor creature neighed painfully and reared up on its hind legs.

The assassin shot Thrax a malevolent glare with his one eye, then cracked his whip to urge his horse on. The poor creature moved like Pegasus escaping from the Chimera's deadly breath. Thrax followed, and the two horses plunged along the narrow streets of the Kerameikos and through the city gates, scattering people in their wake.

This was the road that led to Athena's sacred grove, and Thrax assumed Centaur Alpha was heading there. But, passing some fields beyond the cemetery, the Spartan pulled on the reins and his horse dropped to a trot. He turned up a country lane with vineyards on both sides. It was now dawn and the countryside was bathed in a roseate glow.

Thrax slowed down his horse too. His well-honed instinct for survival told him he was being led into a trap, but he followed Centaur Alpha along the country lane. He passed through a grove of weeping willows, whose branches blocked his view. When he came out of it, there was no sign of Centaur Alpha. His horse was drinking at a slow-moving river.

Thrax stopped at once, his whole body taut with tension. Suddenly he heard a loud grunt and Centaur Alpha dropped down from the branches overhead. Thrax felt the cold tip of a dagger press into his throat.

'We meet once again, boy.'

'Get that knife away from my throat.' As he squirmed in the Spartan's grasp, Thrax dug his heels into his horse's flanks. The horse reared up, throwing both Thrax and Centaur Alpha to the ground. They rolled in the grass.

'Why do you vex me so, boy?' growled Centaur Alpha, the tip of his dagger still pricking Thrax's neck.

'I believe you stole a precious object from a house on the Street of the Four Winds. I've been instructed to bring you to justice.'

'Look at you,' growled the Spartan. 'A downtrodden slave who must walk the streets with a shaved head. What do you owe the rich of Athens?'

'I owe them nothing, sir.'

'A capable, intelligent young man like you.' Centaur Alpha purred like a deadly tiger. 'You are wasted in Athens. What is there for you to do in a city obsessed with theatre and sculpture? Come with me to Sparta. I shall let you grow into a real hero, a man with no limits of endurance. A demi-god.'

'I am not free to roam yet, sir,' said Thrax. 'I belong to Master Ariston the poet.'

'The power of Athens is finished,' continued Centaur Alpha. 'Even as your foolish Pericles wastes the city's time and money on public buildings and grand festivals, your fighting forces grow weak and your coffers run empty.'

'Pericles must not be so useless if you are out to kill him, sir.'

'I admit the general has the gift of the gab. He can speak like a god and while he is in power he can get the Athenians to do anything he wants. But without him, Athens is like a ship without a rudder, a doomed oracle without the pythia. There is going to be a war. Sparta will win and it will come to dominate the Hellenic world. Athens will be forgotten.'

'Athens' coffers are not so empty,' said Thrax. 'Isn't that what your men were after? The bullion hidden in the attic of the Parthenon, and the gold on the statue of Athena? I scouted round the hill under the Acropolis while trying to find a way in. Your men had left all sorts of clues as to your intentions. Ropes hanging from the rocks here and there. Footprints in the soil. The murmur of men hidden in caves, waiting for your signal to attack. The shadow of the centaur projected on the wall of the Parthenon. An audacious and cunning plan, sir, I have to say. Rob Athens so it will not be able to afford ships and weapons to defend itself for a war with Sparta.'

Centaur Alpha smiled. 'You are wasted on these Athenians. Come with me to Sparta. I shall treat you as my son, my own flesh and blood. I shall make you a free man. You will inherit all my wealth.'

'I have all the wealth I need already, sir,' said Thrax. 'I have my friends and my health and perhaps my mother waiting at home for me when I'm free. I have my dignity.'

'Pah,' snorted Centaur Alpha, and the tip of his dagger dug deeper into Thrax's neck, drawing blood. 'You are not so clever after all.'

Thrax laughed. 'I am as clever as you, sir. You think you lured me into a trap but I have laid one of my own.'

Centaur Alpha looked up from his dagger to see a freckled face with spiky hair grinning down at him.

'This is my friend Akademus,' said Thrax. 'He followed us all the way from Athens and

I've been killing time with you while he caught up with us. Where did you borrow the horse, Akademus?'

Akademus giggled. 'A farm outside the walls. I'll take him back as soon as I can.'

'Akademus is only a street child,' Thrax said to Centaur Alpha, 'but I assure you he's lethal with a slingshot.'

Centaur Alpha barely had time to growl before he heard a whooshing sound and a pebble from Akademus's slingshot knocked him out cold.

CHAPTER TWENTY FOUR

Thrax Explains It All

Chytroi, the third night of the Anthesteria

It was late in the afternoon, the same day that Akademus had knocked Centaur Alpha out cold with his infamous slingshot. The rest of Thrax's ragamuffin friends from the agora had secretly followed their leader on a donkey cart. They had trussed up the Spartan and delivered him to the police in Athens. Now the would-be assassin was in custody, awaiting trial. We were gathered in Zeno's andron, waiting to hear Thrax explain how he'd solved the mystery.

Zeno was there, of course, and Master Ariston, who had brought Gaia and his replacement scribe. Socrates had arrived with yet another bruise on his forehead. 'Fell down the stairs this morning,' he said. 'Xanthippe and I have made a deal. She stops throwing pots and I stay out of the house less.'

'I have invited General Pericles too,' said Zeno. 'And Phidias the sculptor.'

'General Pericles will never show up…' began Master Ariston.

But just then we heard a murmur in the courtyard and Hilarion showed in both the general and the sculptor. We all leaped to our feet.

'At ease, gentlemen,' said Pericles. 'I come as a friend, to hear young Thrax speak.' He smiled at Thrax, who was sitting on a stool in the middle of the andron. 'Your master has told me all about you and I'm keen to learn how you came to uncover the Spartan plot.'

Master Ariston made space on the couch for the general and Hilarion went to fetch wine and bowls of honey-coated nuts.

'I did not get to the truth on my own, sir,' said Thrax. 'My friend Nico the scribe was a great help, as was my friend Gaia.'

'Yes,' agreed Pericles, 'she was protesting your innocence even when the rest of the crowd was still against you. A very brave girl.'

Gaia blushed to hear the great Pericles himself sing her praises. She smiled shyly.

'But tell me how you came to discover, and ultimately foil, the Spartan plot,' Pericles said to Thrax.

'It started like this,' volunteered Master Ariston. 'I was invited to a symposium held by Menelaus the goat merchant. I took Thrax and Nico with me and there we met Zeno and Socrates. I told them how clever Thrax is and how many mysteries he and Nico have solved.'

'Zeno was puzzling over a little mystery that had happened in his own house, sir,' Thrax continued. 'It seemed a pointless crime without any motive, which had left him scratching his head in bewilderment.'

'And what was the crime?' asked Pericles.

'Zeno's wife has a dog, sir,' said Thrax. 'A Melitan called Argos.'

'After the hero Odysseus's dog,' pointed out Master Ariston. 'He's adorable.'

'Their slave, Hilarion, was walking the dog one evening, sir,' continued Thrax, 'when he was brutally attacked and the dog was stolen.'

'Goodness,' said Pericles. 'How upsetting for Hilarion and Zeno's wife.'

'Except the dog was returned unharmed the very next day,' said Thrax.

'Do you mean the dog escaped and found its way home?' asked Pericles.

'No, sir. Its lead was tied to the door handle. Whoever had returned the dog wanted to make sure the owner found it.'

'How peculiar,' said Pericles. He turned to Zeno. 'I agree with you; it's a pointless crime.'

'There's no such thing, sir,' said Thrax. 'No crime is pointless. There's always a motive and this had a very important one. Melitans might look small and fluffy, but their barking is both ferocious and persistent. They make extremely good guard dogs. I was of the opinion that someone wanted Argos out of the way for the night.'

'Do you mean someone wanted to break into Zeno's house and steal something without Argos rousing the household?' asked Pericles.

'But nothing was taken from my house, of that I'm sure,' insisted Zeno.

'That's where you're wrong, sir,' said Thrax. 'Something *was* stolen from your house, but we'll come to that in a moment. My first theory was that the thief paid or convinced someone to get rid of the dog for the night, sneaked into the house unaided, and returned the dog in the morning.'

'But why bother returning it?' Pericles wanted to know. 'Why not just get rid of it?'

'Because my first theory was wrong. The thief did not come into the house unaided. The only way in is through a chicken coop at the back of the storeroom, and I know from a handprint he left behind that he was too big to fit through the hole. No, the thief had help from inside the house. Someone let him in.'

'You don't mean someone from my own household?' gasped Zeno. 'Why would they want to help a burglar?'

'Slaves often have to do things they do not want to do,' said Thrax. 'Sir, if I tell you who helped the thief will you promise not to punish them?'

'By the might of Herakles, I give you my word,' answered Zeno without hesitation.

'It was Hilarion,' said Thrax. 'The thief blackmailed him into helping him.'

'How?' asked Socrates.

'The thief knew a secret about Hilarion that he threatened to reveal unless he got the help he needed. I made enquiries with the neighbours and discovered that the slave came with the house when Master Zeno bought it. It was Hilarion who suggested to Zeno that he should buy Eirene the cook. You see, Hilarion and Eirene are secretly man and wife and still very much in love. Nico and I saw Hilarion buying jasmine-scented perfume and the next day I smelled it on Eirene. They married without their owner's permission and had children. As you know, the children of slaves are the property of their owners, to be sold off at will. Hilarion and Eirene could not bear to see their children growing up in bondage, so they gave them up for adoption to people willing to raise them as free citizens. They even have a grandchild, who lives in the care of the priestesses of Hera. The thief threatened to reveal Hilarion's guilty secret, a serious crime in the eyes of the law.'

'But how did the thief know all this?' asked Socrates.

'Because the thief was Hilarion's previous owner, the man who also owned the house before Zeno. He knew Hilarion's secret but rather than give him away to the authorities, he used it to blackmail him.'

'And who returned the dog?' Pericles wanted to know.

'The dog was never stolen, sir,' said Thrax. 'Hilarion's instructions from the thief were to get rid of the dog. But he didn't want to harm it. He knew how much it meant to his mistress and her little son. He simply took it to the priestesses who look after his granddaughter before the thief arrived, and went back for it after he left. The street attack was just a story he made up to explain the dog's disappearance.

'So I concluded that Argos had been removed temporarily in order that he would not bark during the burglary. Then we wanted to know what the thief had stolen.'

'And, needless to say, you discovered that too?' said Master Ariston.

'It did not take me long to find out, sir,' said Thrax. 'Master Zeno's house was built on the ruins of a much more ancient one. Hidden under the floor of this andron is a secret room. It was carved out of the rock when the first house was built, to act as a shelter from pirates and brigands. The man who owned this house before Zeno turned it into a vault to hide his riches. The entrance is marked with a lambda in the mosaic, the sign of the Spartans.'

Zeno looked startled. 'I never knew I was living on top of a secret vault.'

'There is a small altar in the vault,' said Thrax. 'The statue on it was smashed for some reason, but enough of it remained to reveal what it was.'

'And the remains were?' asked Pericles.

'Winged sandals on a pair of feet, sir. The missing statue was Hermes, the god of messengers. And there was a miniature sarcophagus on the altar. It was shaped like a tortoise, the symbol of Hermes. I knew then that whatever had been stolen had something to do with sending a message. I guessed from the indentation left by the missing object in the box that it was a seal. A seal to prove that an important message was actually from the sender.

'So now I knew that an important seal had been stolen. But who had taken it, and what did he need it for?

'I guessed that whoever had helped the thief – at this time I didn't yet know it was Hilarion, just that it was one of the three slaves who'd been in the house the night of the theft – would be rattled if he suspected the crime was going to be discovered. He didn't want the thief to suspect that *he* had given him away, so he would try to make contact with him, to warn him. If I kept an eye on the three slaves, I thought the helper would lead Nico and me to the thief.

'I was right, because Hilarion led us to a flower-picker he met in the gaming room of a tavern. He passed him a note, tied to a petteia pebble. I knew this flower-picker wasn't the thief. He was too slight to have left the handprint in the vault and he most likely couldn't read the note. I figured he was a go-between. The note was intended for someone else.'

'Well I never,' cried Socrates.

'I started shadowing the flower-picker, who is called Zeus, and he led me to the real thief.' Thrax turned to Zeno. 'Do you know who owned this house before you, sir?'

'I bought it from the courts,' said Zeno. 'They did not divulge the identity of the previous owner.'

'The house passed through several hands,' explained Thrax. 'But the man who owned the house before you was a Spartan who came from a long line of wine merchants. Despite his success in Athens, his heart remained loyal to Sparta. I believe he was suspected of treachery against Athens and was ostracised a few years ago. He now lives in a district in the north of Attica called the Acharnian, like the gate at the start of the road that leads to it.'

Thrax took a sip of water and continued. 'In his new home, the Spartan's hate towards Athens grew stronger by the day. One of his ancestors had set up a secret society dedicated to making Sparta the ruling polis in the world. It was called the Secret Society of Centaurs, because centaurs are powerful and when they are angry they can greatly damage, even destroy, their opponents.

'Nico, Gaia and I overheard the centaurs plotting in the sacred grove of Athena to overthrow Athens. They had been waiting for permission from King Archidamus of Sparta, and on the first day of the Anthesteria the permission came.

'Now I knew who the thief was, and why he needed the seal so badly. It was to convince King Archidamus that his letter asking for permission to strike was really from him. You see, the seal was a precious family heirloom that the thief had brought with him from Sparta. He had kept it in the vault for safekeeping and when he was ostracised, he didn't have the opportunity to retrieve it. So he had no choice but to break into his old house and steal it back.'

'And what was the plot against Athens?' asked Zeno.

'Their main intention was to assassinate General Pericles. Then Sparta would declare war and Athens would find itself without a leader to protect it,' replied Thrax. 'But Nico, Gaia and I were determined to foil their plot. We knew the police would not believe our fantastical story, so we had to take matters into our own hands.'

'That's why you wanted my help with getting into the Acropolis,' exclaimed Socrates.

'Exactly,' said Thrax. 'Unfortunately that didn't work out, but we still found our way in. And when Pericles boasted about the gold bullion in the attic, I knew there was another string to the centaur's bow. They wanted to steal the gold from the Parthenon, both the statue of Athena *and* the bullion. There were Spartans hidden in the caves and tunnels under the Acropolis, waiting for a signal to attack: a shadow of a centaur projected on to the temple by a shadow-artist. Had the plot succeeded, it would have been a double blow for the morale of Athens, which would have left it weak and unable to fight when Sparta declared war.'

'Thanks to you, the centaurs' plot failed. I take it the man your friends brought into custody is the leader of the gang,' said Soctrates.

'Centaur Alpha, he calls himself, sir,' I said.

'His real name is Lelex of Sparta,' Pericles informed us. 'One of the prison officials recognised him when he was brought in. Returning to Athens while ostracised is a crime punishable by death. We shall deal with the traitor according to the law and round up the people who helped him, including the infamous shadow-thrower.'

Thrax reached under his belt. 'One of my friends is an expert purse-snatcher. He can remove anything from under a person's belt or from inside his purse without the victim even knowing. He taught me the basics of his skills, and I managed to lift the seal from Lelex of Sparta while I was wrestling with him in the grass. I believe it is rightfully yours, Master Zeno. You bought the house and all the contents in it.'

Thrax held out the seal for all of us to see. It was no bigger than an obol but it flashed on the palm of his hand like a polished gemstone. Carved in it was a minute image of a centaur holding a club over his head. Such a small thing, I thought, which has caused such a lot of trouble.

'There's your case solved, Zeno,' said Socrates. 'Ariston was right. The boy is a genius. Now you must pay him.'

'I couldn't have done it without Nico and Gaia,' protested Thrax.

But the adults were in no mood to listen. Zeno called for more wine and thrust a purse into Thrax's hand. 'Thank you, young man. You have done your master proud.' When Hilarion appeared, Zeno took his hand in his. 'I hold no grudge for what you did. You had no choice. I forgive you, and I relinquish all rights over your children and grandchildren.'

There were tears in Hilarion's eyes as he bent to kiss his master's hand. 'The gods protect you for evermore, master.'

Pericles stood up. 'It is time for me to be generous too.'

He turned to me. 'I know you are a scribe. I shall organise it so that you have a lifetime supply of pens and papyrus to write on. It is Athens' way of showing its gratitude for helping to save my life.

Then the general did something none of us in that room thought we'd ever see him do. He unbuckled the strap under his chin and took off his helmet, exposing his sloping forehead. It was shiny with sweat. 'Come forward, young man,' he said to Thrax. 'And you, Gaia.'

Thrax stood up right away and Gaia came forward only a moment later, her chin jutting out to show she was being brave. Perciles placed a hand on each of their shoulders.

'In the name of the city and polis of Athens and by the powers invested in me by the Athenian assembly, I grant you, Thrax from Thrace and you, Gaia from Corinth, freedom from slavery and the power to live your lives according to your own wishes and ambitions, and in honour of the gods. The city treasury will recompense your masters for their loss. Let this be done in recognition of your brave actions that have saved Athens from its enemies. Let those here present and Athena, protector of the city, be my witnesses. So I have said, so let it be done.'

I saw a look come into Thrax's eyes that I had never seen before. A look of pure joy and sheer relief. I guess Gaia was too young to fully understand what had just happened to her. She merely smiled and shyly slipped her hand in mine. Thrax nodded for me to come forward.

'General, sir, I thank you with all my heart. Like all slaves I have always dreamed of freedom. That it should come so early in my

life is a blessing indeed. I shall go to Thrace in search of my mother, whom I last saw the night I was taken from her. Before I depart, I have one request. My friend Nico is a truly gifted writer. Might you do him the honour of listening to one of his stories before I go?'

'Of course,' said Pericles. 'I shall listen with pleasure.'

Socrates rose to his feet. 'We shall do better than a private reading. I promised this boy that he could come to my house and I would listen to his stories. Well, tonight is the last night of the Anthesteria and I have some guests coming to celebrate the closing of the festival. No theatrical performances are allowed on the day of Chytroi but we must have entertainment, and there is no reason why it should not be a reading. Why don't you all join me and watch Nico perform his professional debut?'

CHAPTER TWENTY FIVE

The Good Ship *Calliope*

Chytroi, the third and last day of the Anthesteria

I stood alone behind a flimsy curtain with a key pattern round the edge, my heart beating in my chest like a festival drum. I could see through it into Socrates' andron. All the couches were full and I knew that many famous people had come to see me perform my first public reading. Pericles was there, his helmet firmly back on his head. So was Euripides the playwright, whom Thrax and I had got to know in Corinth. He'd brought another playwright with him, Sophocles, and the historian Herodotus, my favourite writer even if he had only written one book. Most importantly my friends were there: Thrax and Gaia and Fotini.

The evening had started with the closing ceremony of the Anthesteria. Socrates' cooks had prepared bowls of stewed fruit and lentils. They were not for the guests to eat. They carried them to Hermes at a makeshift altar where they begged the god to keep us safe from the dead and to send them back to the underworld.

Socrates then opened his front door where the patch of tar had dried. 'The Anthesteria is over,' he called out, hurling the stewed fruit and pulses into the street. 'I implore you, souls of the dead, have one last meal and be gone. Return to the underworld and let the living live.'

The ceremony over, it was time for the entertainment. I heard the guests' footsteps returning to the andron. To tell the truth I was really scared as I stood in the shadows, waiting to go on, and I would have loved nothing better than to slip out through the back door and head to the agora for a giant snack. My head swirled with doubts. What if the audience thought my writing second-rate? What if people failed to laugh at the jokes or to thrill to the exciting passages? Cowardly, I thought of feigning a sore throat or a headache. But then Pericles's shadow fell across the curtain and it was too late to back out.

'Ladies and gentlemen,' he announced. 'You all know that two young men and a girl saved my life yesterday. They also saved Athens' reputation and its war chest. They are brave heroes indeed.'

The audience cheered and wine cups were raised. 'Hear! Hear!'

'Two of those heroes turned out to be slaves and I have granted them their freedom. The other is a writer, a very gifted one I'm assured by none other than Socrates the philosopher, and he is the entertainment at our symposium tonight. Ladies and gentlemen, I give you Nico the scribe.'

The slaves parted the curtain and I stepped through into the light of a hundred lamps, and towards the smiling faces of my first audience.

It was difficult to recite at first. Tension made my throat dry and the scroll trembled in my hands. But then I looked at Fotini's smiling face, at Gaia beside her and Thrax nodding encouragingly from a couch. Gaia was dressed in a fabulous chiton, a present from Fotini, with a glittering pin at the shoulder. It was the first time I'd seen Thrax sitting down at a symposium, a free man, and I knew everything was going to be fine.

I relaxed.

The words started to flow and they carried my listeners with them. Through my writing, they joined Thrax and me as we battled hoodlums in a graveyard outside Corinth. They hurtled with us on a ramshackle raft along an underground river in Delphi. They battled the monster Charybdis near the island of Aegina. And I could tell from the silence in the room that they were hanging on to my every word, that I had them in the palm of my hand. I wanted the feeling to last for ever.

As I took my bow at the end of the reading, Socrates, Euripides and Herodotus all rose to their feet and held up their kylix. 'To Nico, the finest adventure writer in Athens.'

Master Ariston joined them, followed by the rest of audience and my three closest friends – 'To Nico, the finest adventure writer in the world.'

It was the best moment of my life.

After the summer comes the rain, after joy sadness, and so it was that night. It was time to say goodbye to Thrax. He was leaving for Thrace at dawn. His bag was packed, his passage purchased with the money from Zeno's payment. He had already taken his leave of Master Ariston and Master Lykos.

Fotini had obtained permission to remain out of the temple after sundown and the four of us walked together to the agora. The last night of the Anthesteria was over and the streets were littered with discarded flowers. The stale smell of their crushed petals mixed with the less intoxicating aroma of thrown-away street food and burnt cooking oil. 'That was the most exciting

Anthesteria ever,' I said. 'And the most dangerous. I can't wait for it to come around again next year.'

Thrax had sent word to Akademus that we wanted to speak to him, and the boy was waiting for us near the fountain of Hera.

'Akademus, this our friend Fotini,' said Thrax. 'You haven't met her because she has been at the temple this last week, but she is a member of our secret society. The Medusa League.'

'A secret society? You mean a gang like the one I'm in?' said Akademus.

'A little like that,' said Thrax. 'But we help to solve crimes and bring criminals to justice.'

'It doesn't sound a very exciting society,' muttered Akademus.

'But it is,' replied Thrax. 'Its members have all sorts of exciting adventures and they help people too.'

'Like I helped you yesterday,' said Akademus.

'Yes, exactly like that,' I said, taking over from Thrax. 'General Pericles was very impressed with your contribution. He sent you this.'

I held out a fat purse bulging with coins.

Akademus's eyes grew wide. 'Say thank you to the general for me. There's enough here to feed all the kids in the agora for a month – and some left over for me to buy a petasos. I hate going out in the sun without a hat.'

Fotini pulled a medallion of the Medusa from her bag. 'Akademus,' she said, 'we would like you to become a member of our secret society and help us solve more crimes. Thrax is not going to be with us for a while and we're going to need the help of some very clever people like you. Would you like that? This is our lucky charm.'

Akademus took the medallion and hung it carefully around his neck. 'Yes, I would be honoured to join the Medusa League. I will wear the medallion with pride. Thank you.'

His fingers ran along the purse that now hung at his belt. I knew he was itching to start spending some money. 'We have to go now,' I said, 'but we'll let you know when the Medusa League needs your help.'

'You can always ask for me at the baker's in the southern stoa,' replied Akademus. 'Have a

safe journey, Thrax. Come back and see us soon.'
He turned to walk away, whistling loudly.

We watched him disappear into the thinning crowd. Usually inducting a new member to the Medusa League is a joyous occasion. But tonight we all felt sad. We were about to say goodbye to our most important member.

Thrax's ship was sailing from Piraeus, the main port in Athens we had often used before. Thrax, Gaia and I walked him all the way there, along a wide road protected from pirates and invaders by high walls. The seagulls wheeled and cawed above us and a stiff breeze blew in from the sea. The morning sky turned a pearly grey, then pink.

It was going to be the perfect day for sailing. We asked for directions and found his ship berthed at the dock. It was a small merchant vessel called the *Calliope*.

'Thrax,' I said before he got on board. 'Do you remember after our first adventure in Corinth, we released a dove and you said "one day I will be free as that bird"? Well, now you are.'

'I am,' he said. 'And I couldn't have done it without your help, Nico. Thank you.' He pulled his purse out of his bag. 'We earned quite a bit of money to buy my freedom but in the end we didn't use it. Here, Nico. Take the money.'

I pushed the purse away. 'Keep it,' I said. 'You might need it to buy your mother's freedom if she was enslaved at the same time as you.'

Thrax smiled. 'I can't believe I'm off to look for her at last. I have dreamed of this moment as long as I can remember,'

'Keep in mind what Selene told you in Delphi,' I said. 'Your mother is waiting for you. You will find her.'

'And then I'll bring her to Athens to meet you all.'

The ship's first mate called from the deck. 'All aboard, please. We're casting out. All aboard.'

'If I have found my freedom, Nico, you have found your calling,' said Thrax. 'Last night was a big step for you. Your first public reading.'

'And it all happened because of you.'

'No, you were always a writer,' said Thrax. 'You just needed someone to push you in the right direction.'

The ship's first mate called again. 'All aboard now. All aboard. The good ship *Calliope* is sailing.'

We all hugged Thrax goodbye while other travellers clambered aboard and the sailors offered sacrifice to Poseidon for a safe journey. I'd always wished Thrax would come to this moment but now that it had arrived, I had to admit my heart was breaking. Saying goodbye is much more painful than you think.

In a quick blur of movement, the anchor was lifted, the rowers set to and the *Calliope* slipped away fromg the quay. Fotini, Gaia and I waved at Thrax till the ship was just a speck on the ocean and we couldn't see him any more.

'May Poseidon and Athena go with him and bless him all the way,' said Gaia.

'And may Hera reunite him with his mother,' added Fotini.

'Yes,' I said, 'and may she bring him home safely. I know he'll be back one day. We'll have more adventures and more mysteries to solve. The Medusa League will be strong again. Meanwhile I have another story to write, one that might please my new audience even more than the adventures I recounted at my debut. I already have a title for it: *Shadow of the Centaurs*.'

Bonus Bits!

Greek gods and myths

Thrax and Nico, the main characters in our story, lived in a period of Greek history known as Classical Greece. It lasted from around 510 to 323 BC. The age when myth and history merged was long gone. People still believed in the ancient gods, though. They prayed and sacrificed to them often and referred to them all the time. Here is a list of gods and some mythical characters mentioned in our story.

Aphrodite   goddess of love and beauty. Her special symbol was the evening star. She was also associated with the sea and was often depicted in art swimming with dolphins and swans or surrounded by pearls.

Apollo god of music and poetry. A beautiful young man, his symbol was the lyre. When only four days old, Apollo was believed to have killed a serpent-like dragon called the Phyton.

Ares god of war. One of the twelve Olympians, the ancient Greeks considered him dangerous. He drove a war chariot through the skies, accompanied by his children Phobos, the god of fear and Deimos, the god of terror. His symbols included the shield, the spear and the vulture.

Argonauts group of brave sailors and heroes who, according to Greek myth, sailed with Jason to Colchis. They were named after their ship, the Argo. Their journey is meant to have taken place around 1300 BC. Among them were the hero Herakles and his nephew Iolaus.

Argos dog made famous by the ancient Greek author Homer in his masterpiece, The Odyssey. He belonged to the hero Odysseus and waited for him to return home from the Trojan war. He was known for his speed and strength.

Ariadne a princess, daughter of King Minos. She was in charge of the sacrifices offered to Poseidon in the Minotaur's labyrinth. She helped Theseus kill the Minotaur and then find his way out of the maze. As she was travelling to Athens with the prince, Dionysus fell in love with her and carried her away to Mount Olympus.

Athena goddess of many things, including wisdom, mathematics, war and heroes. She was also the goddess who protected Athens, her city. Her many symbols included the owl, the olive tree, the shield, the spear and a protective amulet with the Medusa's face on it.

Centaurs mythical creatures, part horse and part human being. To the ancient Greeks, they represented cruelty. At least one of them, however, was considered wise and gentle. His name was Chiron and he was the tutor to the god Asklepios and the heroes Herakles, Achilles and Jason.

Charon ferryman who carried the souls of the dead to Hades, the underworld.

Charybdis mythical sea monster that lived under a rock in the sea. Ancient sailors believed it swallowed colossal amounts of water three times a day, which it spat out to create a deadly whirlpool.

Demeter goddess of the earth, the harvest and fertility. She was also the patron of sacred law. Bakers always sacrificed the first loaf of bread made with new corn to her. Her symbols were the torch, bread, sheaves of wheat and the cornucopia.

Dionysus god of wine, the grape harvest, merrymaking, theatre and ritual madness. Many illustrations of him show him as a well-rounded old man but he is sometimes drawn as a younger person too. He was looked after by magical rain nymphs when he was a child.

Hades god of the underworld, which was called after him. He was also the god of darkness, death, the afterlife and metal. People were often too scared to call him by name, in case he came to fetch them to the underworld.

Hera the mother goddess. She was married to Zeus, the chief god, and was protector of women, marriage and the family. Believed to be a very serious person, she was often depicted on a throne. The peacock, the cow and the lily were some of her many symbols.

Herakles son of Zeus and a famous hero in Greek mythology. When he killed his wife and children by mistake, the god Apollo set him twelve tasks. If he performed them all, not only would he be forgiven but he'd also become a god himself. When the mortal part of him died, Zeus himself sent a chariot to fetch Herakles to Olympus.

Hermes god of thieves, travellers and athletes. Believed to be quick on his feet and able to slip easily from the mortal world into the mystical one, he acted as a messenger for the other gods. He was also honoured as the god of boundaries between countries and worlds.

Jason mythical prince whose father was killed by his own half- brother, King Pelias. When he tried to reclaim his throne, his uncle sent him to fetch the fabled golden fleece from the faraway land of Colchis. King Pelias thought Jason would never return but he did.

Medusa a gorgon, a monster with snakes for hair. If anyone looked into her eyes, they were turned immediately to stone. Medusa had two sisters who were immortal. They could not be killed. The hero Perseus managed to cut off Medusa's head. He escaped being turne to stone by only looking at the gorgon's reflection in his shield.

Odysseus a king and one of the heroes of the Trojan War. He had the idea to build a wooden horse in which the Greeks hid until they were taken into Troy. He was known for his wisdom and courage. His journey home after the war was filled with adventures involving storms, monsters and wicked spells.

Pan god of shepherds and hunters. He also protected the forests and the medows. In art, he was always shown as a man with the horns, tail and legs of a goat. He also had a very thick beard and pointy ears. Pan played the pipes, always hidden from the view of mortals. He liked chasing nymphs.

Persephone Demeter's daughter. When she was kidnapped by Hades, she also became queen of the underworld. Her symbols were the pomegranate, seeds, torches and deer. She was often seen in statues carrying a musical instrument called a systrum. Sometimes she was also shown carrying a sheaf of corn.

Poseidon god of the sea. He was also known as the earth-shaker because he could cause eathquakes. He could create islands and springs by striking rocks with his trident. Sailors prayed to him for protection while fishermen left their tridents in his temple when they retired.

Zeus the chief god on Mount Olympus and ruled over the other gods with a fiery temper. All the other gods rose to their feet when he was present. His special symbols were the oak, the bull and the thunderbolt – which he loved hurling at his enemies. He was married to Hera.

GLOSSARY

Thrax and Nico use many Greek words in their fourth adventure. Here is a list of what they mean.

Agora   a meeting place for a town or city. It was also a market place

Amis   a chamber pot. It was kept close to or under a bed so people did not have to go to the bathroom in the middle of the night

Andron   a special room where men relaxed and held parties

Anthesteria   an annual festival held in ancient Athens. One of the four festivals, dedicated to the god Dionysus, it took place on the 11th, 12th and

13th of the month known as Anthesterion. That would be in January or February in our calendar

Attica   a region in Greece that surrounds the city of Athens

Aulos   a musical instrument made with two reed pipes

Bouleuterion   a building in ancient Greece where the council met

Chalkoi   a Greek coin of small value. Eight chalkoi were worth one obol

Chiton   a long tunic, usually made of wool

Chlamys   a short woollen cloak

Deme   a zone or suburb of a city or region

Discus   heavy disc used in sport

Doric   a simple form of design in architecture

Epiblema   a shawl, usually worn by women, especially if they had sleeveless clothes on

Fibula   a brooch or a clasp

Gymnasiarch   an athlete who also ran a gym

Gynaikon   the part of a Greek house, usually upstairs, reserved for women

Hellenic   referring to Hellas which was what the ancient Greeks called their world

Himation   a long woollen garment, like a cloak, worn over the left shoulder, usually worn by men

Hoplites   Greek citizens who also acted as soldiers

Kalamos   a reed pen with a hard tip, used for writing on papyrus or parchment

Keramaikos   part of Athens where many potters lived

Kapeleion   a bar that served food and drink

Khaire   ancient Greek word which meant 'rejoice'. It was used like our 'hello'

Klepsydra   a famous spring located under the Acropolis in Athens

Kottabos   a popular game played during symposiums, where players flung wine at a basin

Koudounias   bell-like instruments made of copper. You play them by hitting them with a stick

Krater   a large vase used for mixing wine and water

Krotalas   wooden clappers, a bit like modern castanets

Kylix   a two-handled drinking cup

Lekanis   a small flat pot with a lid, sometimes used for storing make-up

Narcissi   scented wild flowers with white petals

Nymphs   female spirits and minor goddesses of the natural world, who lived in springs, rivers, seas and meadows

Obol a coin. One obol was worth eight chalkoi. In Athens, obols were made of silver

Panoply a suit of armour

Pelike a two-handled jug, usually decorated with beautiful pictures.

Petasos a wide-brimmed sun hat

Petteia a popular board game. The word itself means 'pebbles'

Phalanx a group of soldiers. They fought holding their shields together to create a protective wall

Pithoi large storage containers with two handles used for bulk storage of wine and other goods

Polis an ancient city or city-state

Pythia the priestess of the oracle of Delphi

Propylaea the grand entrance to the Acropolis

Sarcophagus a stone coffin, mostly used in ancient Egypt

Stoa a covered walkway, usually in public places

Styx one of the rivers in the underworld

Symposium a party for men only, with music, entertainment and discussions

Tiganites wheat pancakes, usually eaten for breakfast

Tesserae small pieces of stone used to make a mosaic

Tympanums ancient Greek tambourines

Acknowledgments

As always, I have a few people to thank for helping to bring this story to life and into the hands of my readers. Hannah Rolls at Bloomsbury for being so patient, my editor Susila Baybars and my agent Katy Loffman at Paper Lion.

Thanks are also due to the hundreds of Year 5 and 6 students in Leeds and Bradford schools who listened to early drafts of the story and gave advice.

Did you like *Shadow of the Centaur* or any of the other Ancient Greek Mysteries? Email Saviour and let him know at www.spirotta.com